WORTHLESS TREASURES
A NOVEL

MARY L. HAMILTON

BLUE MIST BOOKS

Worthless Treasures

Copyright March 2025 by Mary L Hamilton

Published by Blue Mist Books

All rights reserved. No part of this publication may be reproduced, digitally stored, or transmitted in any form without written permission from the author.

Scripture taken from the HOLY BIBLE, NEW INTERNATIONAL VERSION®Copyright© 1973,1978,1984 by International Bible Society. Used by permission of Zondervan. All rights reserved.

This story is a work of fiction. While some location names have been included for effect, all characters and places in this novel are fictitious. Any resemblance to real locations or persons, living or dead, is purely coincidental.

Cover design by 100 Covers

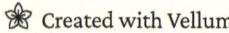 Created with Vellum

For Mom

(and all who struggle with letting go)

The Lord your God has chosen you out of all the people on the face of the earth to be his people, his treasured possession. (Deuteronomy 7:6b, NIV)

1

Diamond Lange could make dust and clutter disappear from any home—except Eva Malone's.

What does one call a professional cleaner/organizer whose own mother's house might be classified as a minor landfill? A failure, that's what.

As Eva's house came into view, Di vowed once again to avoid criticizing Eva's housekeeping habits, or lack of. Such promises had yet to be kept.

Her car rocked over driveway pavement cracked and broken by roots from an ancient live oak tree that shaded the house from the blistering Texas sun. This being the last of April, the summer heat was getting an early start. At least the white siding was in good shape, thanks to her husband Mitch's patching and painting last fall. If only the inside of the house looked as good.

She sighed, grabbed the pharmacy bag from the front seat, and hurried past a struggling azalea bush. The yard looked dry, the grass sparse, especially under the trees, and the beds needed some fresh color. But all that would have to wait. Her next appointment was in forty-five minutes, so this would be a short visit.

Di knocked twice on the front door of the older ranch-style home, steeled herself against the mess inside, then twisted the knob and shouted, "It's me." Eva's increasing difficulty in getting around prompted her to leave the door unlocked so visitors could enter easily. Di prayed no unsavory characters would come to visit. Then again, anyone intending harm to Eva Malone would first have to surmount the obstacle course inside. And the prospect of wading through the debris for anything valuable would certainly deter any thieves.

Di pushed open the door and grimaced at the jam-packed living room. The old piano that took up space but hadn't uttered a purposeful note in decades held piles of outdated magazines, a couple of plastic eggs left over from Easter, and a Christmas snow globe. Newspapers, calendars, and other useless knickknacks littered every square inch and contributed to the odor of dust and mildew. Even the abstract art pieces on the walls looked as if someone had simply framed a drop cloth. But what did she know about art?

Eva, still in her frumpy bathrobe, strained to push her ample body out of her worn recliner with its frayed and thread-bare upholstery. Her arms gave way, sending her back onto the faded seat cushion. She inched forward to the edge and tried again.

"Would you like some help?" Di moved closer to support her efforts. Her heart ached watching Eva struggle. Not so long ago, the woman was a dynamo, hard to keep up with.

Eva waved her off and nearly lost the battle again. "I can" —huff, puff—"do it." She stood upright, as much as her bent frame would allow, and glared at Di. "What happened to Aunt Glori? I thought she was coming."

Di held up the pharmacy bag. "She's showing a house.

Asked me to pick up your medicines. Do you want them here or should I put them in the kitchen?" The bag rattled when she shook it.

"I'll take them." Holding onto the recliner, Eva reached across a footstool stacked with books.

"Aunt Glori said your power is out. Has it been off long?" Di flicked the light switch. Nothing. She tried the lamp beside the recliner, but it remained dark. Despite the outside warmth, the house was a little on the cool side. "Are you chilly? Would you like me to get your sweater?"

Eva waved away the offer and shuffled a few steps to set the bag of medicines on the end table beside her recliner. Pressing one hand to the back of her hip, she straightened to her five-foot height.

"I told Gloria I'd take care of it myself. She wasn't supposed to mention it."

"She's only trying to help, Mother. Mind if I go out and check the breakers?"

"I already looked."

Di doubted Eva would've made it all the way out to the garage, but her mother detested appearing less than competent. "I'm sure you did, but I'll recheck just to be sure. While I'm out there, I'll look around to see if I can figure out what's going on."

Stepping lightly, Di maneuvered around the landmines of papers, books, and other detritus as she proceeded to the kitchen, biting her tongue to keep from starting the familiar argument that never brought about any change. A sour smell emanated from the kitchen. Or had something died? She wrinkled her nose.

Inside the garage, she automatically reached to flip the light switch, then shook her head. *Duh, no power.* She used her phone to light the way around the perimeter of a musty garage as full of junk as the house. A sneezing fit briefly interrupted her progress.

All the breakers were intact, but she flipped each one to be certain. She let herself out the door to the side yard and checked the power line to the house. Nothing appeared amiss, other than a garbage bin on its side. She righted it and returned it to the driveway side of the house. Letting herself in the back door, she wiped her feet on a faded towel and made a mental note to buy a doormat the next time she went to the store. Adding one more thing to an already overflowing house might not be wise but at least a mat was useful. Eva would love one of the cute ones she'd seen at the craft store.

"Everything looks okay. Have you asked any neighbors if they have power?" Di twisted the knob on the electric stove and held her hand above the burner while surveying the messy counter. A white envelope peeked out from under a mound of restaurant and real estate flyers. The envelope bore a red ink stamp that read "Final Notice." Di snatched it from the pile, glanced at the return address, and tore it open.

"Mother? When was the last time you paid your electric bill?" She stumbled through the narrow trail and handed the notice to Eva. "Have you paid this?"

"Of course, I—" Eva backed her head away, adjusted her glasses, and studied the paper. Her forehead wrinkled and she turned away. "Where did you find that? I've been looking all over for it."

"So, you haven't paid it."

Eva scooched down in her recliner. Her gaze darted around the room. "I set it down somewhere, then couldn't find it when I went to write the check. Figured I'd come across it sooner or later."

Di exhaled her frustration. "It was buried under a pile of

advertisements. You wouldn't lose important bills if you'd get rid of all this junk."

"Don't call my stuff junk."

"Restaurant and real estate flyers that you'll never use, or need, are junk." Di picked up a yellowed newspaper from a nearby stool. "And a three-year-old newspaper is junk. Why are you keeping it?"

"There's something in there I want to read." Eva attempted to snatch the paper from her, but Di whipped it behind her back.

"Tell me what it is, and I'll cut it out for you. There's no reason to keep the whole paper for one article."

Eva put a finger to her cheek. "There might have been more than one. I don't remember. I'd have to look through it."

"And when were you planning to do that?"

"As soon as I have time." Eva pushed herself forward to the edge of her chair.

Di's earlier promise not to criticize flitted through her mind. She ignored it when her foot caught on a nearby stack of magazines, and they cascaded in all directions. An old *TV Guide* landed at her feet. Di picked it up and held it out to Eva.

"The information in here is outdated. It's useless and needs to go."

Eva grabbed it and riffled the pages. "I wanted to read the article from the front cover."

Di gritted her teeth. "Mother, how can you live like this?"

Eva jabbed her finger at Di. "You know I don't like being called that."

"And you know I don't like you living in the middle of such a mess."

With more energy than she'd shown earlier, Eva pushed herself up and glared.

"It's my house." She bent over to straighten the magazines,

but halfway down she gripped the arm of the recliner while her other hand went to her lower back. Rising slowly, she said, "I'll get those later."

"This is not a healthy way to live." Di squatted to gather and restack the publications.

"Do I look sick?" Eva patted her Clairol-red hair with its white roots and raised a thickly penciled eyebrow.

"Not all illnesses are obvious. Speaking of which, how's your blood pressure? The pharmacist mentioned your meds have been increased."

Eva's shoulders slouched. "Doc says I need to lose weight, but what does he know? He's not even old enough to drive. How am I supposed to lose weight when it hurts to move?"

Di stared at the *Southern Living* magazine in her hands. Her throat tightened as she considered the difficulties that accompanied Eva's age and health. Squinting at the 2015 date on the magazine, she shook her head and softened her voice.

"What if we cleared out some of this stuff to give you more space? I think you'd be happier with room to move around in."

"Who says I'm not happy?" Eva nudged a stray periodical toward Di with her foot.

Di topped the stack with a *Reader's Digest* and slid the pile farther away from the narrow traffic lane. Arguing only made Eva more obstinate. She'd try a different approach. Brushing the dust from her hands, she motioned for Eva to sit and settled cross-legged on the floor near her feet. Di willed her voice to a conciliatory tone.

"Won't you please let me work with you, Eva? We can at least organize your things so you can find them easier. Other people trust me to do that for them."

Eva sniffed. "Your idea of organizing is throwing things away." She reached back for the armrests and aimed her backside onto the seat of her oversized recliner. "You were always good at making things disappear. You should work with that woman who flips houses."

"Is that all I am? A cleaning lady?" Di quelled her rising irritation. "I'm a businesswoman, Mother, same as the house flipper. I have employees who do the cleaning now. I do the organizing. People hire me to put things in order. Sometimes that does include getting rid of stuff that's no longer useful or necessary."

She pushed aside a pile of folded clothes lying on the couch and moved onto the sagging cushions. The odd assortment of apparel beside her included the red plaid jumper she'd worn for her fifth-grade school picture. Speaking of no longer useful or necessary...

Breathing deep to control her anger, she leaned forward. "I worry about you, Eva. What if you catch your foot on something and fall? You could hit your head, break an arm or a hip. What if you need to get out quickly? All the clutter and junk in here makes the house a real fire hazard."

Pointing an arthritic finger at her, Eva narrowed her eyes. "Leave it alone. When I'm gone, you can throw everything away. But until then, this is my house and my stuff."

"Fine." Palms up in surrender, Di rose to her feet. She was finished. No more arguing. "If that's the way you want it, you can have it."

"This is the way I want it. Although when the time comes, I do have a few things I don't want you to throw away. A few... treasures."

"Like what? The artwork on your walls? Your jewelry?"

"No, I don't care what you do with those. I'll make a list for you. But you must promise you'll give them to people who will cherish them like I do."

A list—as likely to get lost in the mess as the electric bill.

The pharmacy bag caught Di's eye, and a shiver of alarm

passed through her. "Is there something you're not telling me? Did you get bad news from the doctor?"

"Psh." Eva waved away the suggestion. "Nothing like that, but at my age, you just never know." She fixed a steady gaze on Di. "But I want your promise."

If Di had her way right now, she'd throw out the mostly-burned candles, the bag of peppermint candies so old they had melted and stuck together, and the cheap knickknack from the local gift shop that bore a Bible verse. But, she reminded herself, this wasn't her house.

"All right, I promise. But Eva," Di sighed, "this clutter chokes the life out of me. I can't even catch a deep breath." She sucked in as much air as she could. "I'll do what you ask. But if you're not willing to clean all this out, I'll only come back inside this house if it's an emergency."

Eva's eyes glinted and she raised her chin. "If that's the way you want it—"

"It's not the way I want it, Mother. I want to come and spend time with you. But you'd rather have your clutter than your own daughter."

Eva's mouth took on a firm set. "I guess that makes us two of a kind, doesn't it? Neither of us is willing to give up our comfort for the other."

"It's not the same thing, Mother."

"Isn't it?" She shook her finger at Di. "I don't appreciate you coming in here telling me what to do with my own house. What if I did that to you? If it bothers you so much, then just leave."

Thrown out of her own mother's house?

Di stomped to the door and yanked it open. "Do you want me to contact the power company for you?"

"I told Gloria I'd take care of it, and I will. You don't need to do a thing."

Without saying good-bye, Di closed the door firmly and inhaled the fresh air. She mumbled all the way to her car. "House is a death trap. She clings to all that useless junk like it's the gold of Fort Knox." She could almost recite the lines from their repeated arguments, going over the same things time after time.

Was it so unreasonable to expect a 79-year-old woman to change? She shuddered to think of Eva falling, lying alone for hours or days, unable to call for help. Or burning to death in a fire. She resisted even imagining that horror, but she'd never forgive herself if such a tragedy occurred.

People would naturally ask who allowed her to live in such deplorable conditions. What would happen when they found out the person responsible was not only her daughter, but also the owner/operator of Diamond Cleaning and Organizing?

Her hand shook as she pressed the button to start the engine. She hated leaving on such a bitter note. Should she go back in and say a proper good-bye? Maybe even scoot a few more things farther from Eva's path? She recalled Eva's finger pointing and the order to leave it alone.

All right then.

Di backed out of the driveway, realizing for the first time how few neighbors Eva might have called regarding the power. She drove slowly through the neighborhood, the number of vacant houses finally registering in her brain. Torn screens on broken windows, trash strewn in front yards, and spray-painted gang symbols on doors attested to the presence of vandals and those unsavory characters she'd feared.

What had happened to this solid middle-class neighborhood where she grew up? A downturn in the economy had resulted in many of the houses being snapped up by investors who turned them into rentals. Those hadn't been kept up and showed signs of age and neglect. But why were so many now vacant?

With the corresponding rise in crime, Di had begged Eva to move, but she refused to leave the small, three-bedroom home she'd occupied for nearly a half-century. And despite concerns for Eva's safety, Diamond hated the thought of moving all that junk.

Even cleaning ladies had limits.

2

In contrast to the jungle inside Eva's house, the interior of Di's newest client's house felt like a pleasant open meadow.

Alice McCormack led Di into the living room of her large, two-story home in Waco's historic Castle Heights neighborhood. Floor-to-ceiling windows revealed a landscaped yard with colorful flowers in various planters and beds. Inside cushioned chairs formed a cozy semi-circle around the fieldstone hearth. Di stepped between them to examine the matching Oriental tapestries hanging on either side of the fireplace.

A trim, white-haired woman in her 80s, Alice possessed a posture and bearing that left no doubt about her self-confidence, yet without the arrogance and overbearing attitude Di had encountered in a few clients.

"I've decided to move to a condominium in that new retirement community." Alice's jewel-bedecked hand rested on a seat back.

Di turned from the tapestries. "The one that overlooks Lake Waco?"

"Yes. Obviously, I'll need to downsize, and I'd like your help."

"How big is the condo?" Di dug her stockinged toes into the plush white carpeting, having slipped her shoes off at the door.

"It's a two-bedroom, smaller than this first floor. I've offered my children anything they might want but things are so different nowadays. No one wants heavy furniture, fine china, or silver place settings anymore." A frown tugged at the corners of her mouth.

"Giving your kids first choice is a good start. Next, you'll want to make a couple of lists—one for everything you definitely don't want and another for what you do want to take with you."

Alice nodded her understanding, then led the way through a modern kitchen into the formal dining room.

An antique buffet caught Di's attention. "What a beautiful piece of furniture. Is it walnut?"

"Yes, a family heirloom on my husband's side. He passed away last year. Worked for an oil company back when they moved their engineers around every few years."

"I'm sorry about your husband." Di examined the buffet. "Will you be keeping this?"

Alice hesitated, then shook her head. "It wouldn't fit. I'll see if any of his extended relatives might want it."

"If not, I can give you a list of antique and collectible dealers who might give you something for it."

Alice continued up the stairs and pointed out each bedroom and bath as they passed. Di observed the rooms with an eye to assessing the work.

"Was it hard on your family to move around so often?"

"Sometimes, but we enjoyed seeing different parts of the world. And the frequent moves required me to keep our possessions to a minimum. Until he retired and we settled here."

Di stopped to admire a small teardrop-shaped bottle on a dresser. "Is this for perfume?" Gold leaf ringed the bottom and top of the pedestal base while the purple glass body held an etched leaf and berry design. A purple topper rose to a steeple tipped with a clear bead.

"That's from our time in Egypt. It's hand-blown glass." Alice picked it up, pulled out the stopper, and handed the two pieces to Di.

"It's beautiful. So delicate." Di sniffed the bottle but detected no scent.

"You can put perfume in it, but I've only used it for decoration. Keep it if you'd like."

"Oh no." Di replaced the stopper and handed it back, but Alice pushed it away.

"It's not going with me. You appreciate its beauty, so take it."

"But it's small. Are you sure you don't want to keep it?"

"I'll keep the memory of it." Alice smiled, looking pleased with herself. "And if I happen to lose the memory, I won't miss it anyway."

———

Late afternoon sunlight streamed through the kitchen window splashing lilac-colored hues from the perfume bottle across the counters, the leaf pattern distorted in the refracted light. What a difference between Alice and Eva. The two might as well be day and night, summer and winter, ice cream and kale.

Eva's comment about making things disappear came to mind while Di unpacked the groceries she'd picked up on the way home. Not the first time she'd disparaged Di's profession, but it stung. Every time. Di stiffened her shoulders and spoke her rebuttal into the empty kitchen.

"If I hadn't spent half my life cleaning up after you, Eva, maybe I could've accomplished something more worthy of your respect." She plunked the soup cans on the counter with a *thwack*, then wrapped a package of chicken breasts and shoved it into the freezer. Having loaded her arms with as many boxes and cans as she could carry, she entered the walk-in pantry and arranged them on the shelves.

Hmmm. Maybe she should move the soups next to the canned tomatoes. The pasta boxes needed straightening. And what's a can of black beans doing among the pinto beans?

A door slammed.

"Di?" Mitch poked his head into the pantry. "Uh-oh. Re-organizing?"

"Not exactly." She kissed Mitch and quickly relocated the black beans before following him back to the bedroom. "How was your day?"

"I closed two sales, one on a car and the other a pickup. And I made top sales associate again this month."

"Congratulations." She hugged him, and they exchanged another kiss, his breath holding a latent hint of coffee. "Does that mean I can start planning a Hawaiian vacation?"

She loved hearing his laugh. That full-on smile was what first attracted her, along with his sense of humor that took the edge off her tendency to be too serious. Touches of gray traced the dark edges of hair at his temples, giving him a young George Clooney look.

While Mitch exchanged his work pants for running shorts, Di related the story of Eva's power being shut off. She followed behind him, flipping a pant leg that hung over the edge of the hamper and straightening the socks in his drawer.

"I told her I'm not going back unless there's an emergency.

And then she kicked me out of her house." She pushed the drawer closed.

Mitch stopped unbuttoning his shirt and winced. "Are you sure you want to handle it that way? I mean, her health isn't great and she's not getting any younger."

"Her house isn't getting any cleaner, either. She won't listen when I tell her how dangerous it is to live with all that clutter."

Mitch hesitated only a moment. "You do know your perfectionism is showing, right?" He shrugged out of his shirt and tossed it in the hamper.

"I'm not a perfectionist. I just like things neat. And I'm so frustrated." She adjusted one of his shirts so it hung evenly on the hanger. "Be glad I'm not into retail therapy."

"Oh, I'm very happy about that. But if you don't like going into her house, I think you'll need to take her out. Often. For a meal or a show or something. Anything. You don't want to regret this when she's gone for good."

"Well, that's a cheery thought." A niggle of conviction made her pause. "Yeah, you're right. I'll call tomorrow and see if she wants to go for lunch on Saturday."

A door slammed again, and Julianna called out, "Mom? Dad?"

"We're back in the bedroom." Di stifled a groan. "Doesn't anyone in this family know how to close a door softly?"

Mitch grinned and bent over to tie the laces on his running shoes. "Only two years before she's off to college. Then you'll miss those slamming doors."

Julianna bounded into the room, dropped her backpack, and threw her arms in the air. "I'm up for the lead role in the children's theater production."

"Congratulations!" Di applauded. "Is this for Cinderella?"

Julianna nodded, but her expression clouded. "It's between

Briana and me. She'd be fantastic, but her parents are threatening to make her drop out of the play because of her grades. I feel so bad for her."

"That is a shame," Di said, "but grades are lots more important than a play."

"I know." Julianna bit her lip. "But if she has to drop out, I get the part." A smile returned to her face and her feet did a happy dance. "Can you imagine me as Cinderella?"

Mitch walked over, hugged her, and planted a kiss on her forehead. "If you need to do any research for this role, I'm sure Mom has some floors that need mopping. You could clean out the fireplace ashes, sweep the garage—"

"Da-ad." Julianna swatted at his arm, but he sidestepped and headed for the door.

"I'm going out for a run. Back before supper. Make sure it's on time, Cinderella."

Di pointed to the door and she and Julianna chorused, "Go!"

Julianna bounced on her toes. Her chestnut-colored ponytail bobbed and swished across her shoulders. "I'm so excited, Mom. If I do well, I'll have a good chance of getting more parts, maybe even acting in one of the adult productions."

"Think you can handle practices with homework?"

"I'll make it work. I've dreamed of a starring role since forever." She hugged herself then ran to answer the doorbell. "I'll get it. It's probably Namiko. Wait 'til I tell him."

Di stared after her daughter, listening to her excited report and the soft response of her latest boyfriend.

Absently, she fingered the diamond on her necklace, a gift from her parents when she was around Julianna's age. Had she entertained such grand dreams at that age? Or had she been too much of a Cinderella, working hard to stay ahead of Eva's clutter? Maybe Mother was right. She could've done more than organizing people's homes, if only she'd learned to flip houses rather than clean them.

"Is it too much to ask a nearly 80-year-old to change a habit they've had for most of their life?" Standing in the doorway of their ensuite bathroom, Di spoke through the mint foam in her mouth and waved her toothbrush in the air. "I mean, she's been like this to some extent as far back as I can remember. Dad helped keep it in check when he was alive, but after he passed away, the mess kept expanding, creeping into every room, every corner." She hurried to rinse her mouth while Mitch headed for the bed.

"Could it be related to the depression you said she was treated for after he died?" Mitch pulled back the pale green duvet and climbed into bed. The lamp on the nightstand cast a soft glow over his reading glasses and a couple of books that Di kept trying to relocate to the bookcase. He plumped the pillow behind him and relaxed against it, spreading his arm toward Di.

"Maybe, but I think it's more than that." She snuggled in beside him, catching a whiff of the sporty soap he showered with. "I was always a little embarrassed to have friends over because of the mess. But they all loved Eva and never said anything about it. She always excused it, saying creativity is messy and, as an artist, she couldn't help it. Now they say it's a mental health issue, related to obsessive-compulsive disorders."

Mitch yawned. "It's amazing she stayed organized enough to teach her classes at the university. Must've been creative enough to wing it."

"Or she had taught so long she simply knew what to do."

She turned her head and gazed up at him. His eyes were closed, but his breathing wasn't the slow, steady pace of sleep. And his arm hadn't yet relaxed around her.

"I noticed another vacant house a couple of blocks from Eva's. The gangs have already claimed it. I wish I could persuade her to move."

"That would upset all her stuff." He opened his eyes and met her gaze. "But she may not have a choice. One of the women in our sales office owns a rental in that neighborhood. She says a redevelopment plan is in the works."

Di pulled away and sat up straight. "As in tearing down the old houses and building big fancy new ones?"

"Something like that. Has Aunt Glori mentioned anything about it?"

"Not a word."

"I wonder if she even knows. According to Yvonne, it's all been rather hush-hush. When I said my mother-in-law lived over there, she asked how much they offered her."

Di blinked. "Eva hasn't mentioned any offers, but I doubt she would've accepted no matter how much they promised. She has enough to live on, and that's the home she and Dad bought when they were young-marrieds."

"Yvonne says the powers-that-be held a meeting with homeowners to discuss the plans, but by then all the permits had been approved. She claims the meeting was merely a courtesy to let everyone know what was coming and give them time to sell out on their own."

Di pondered the news. "I hate to think of our long-time neighbors and friends being displaced. The few who still live there are elderly like Eva."

"But it could be the opportunity you're looking for to get Eva into a safer neighborhood. If her house is within the boundary of the development, she'll have to move by a certain deadline. And that way, you won't be the bad guy forcing her to leave her house." His arm still outstretched, Mitch wiggled his fingers, inviting her back, and she snuggled into him again.

"It's sad to imagine the house, the community where I grew up all gone."

Mitch bent his head toward her. "I thought you'd be happy. You wanted her house cleaned out."

"Cleaned, yes. Not destroyed. Isn't there anything we can do to stop it? Protest to the mayor or someone?"

"Yvonne and her husband checked into it but, as far as they can tell, everything was done within regulations. It's all settled. You could try complaining to the city council, but I doubt it would do any good at this point."

"You know I'd love to get Eva out of there, but this seems so wrong. The elderly have no power against progress and development. If I were mayor, I'd—" Now there was an idea that would elevate her status from lowly cleaning woman. "Maybe that's what I should do."

Mitch threw back his head and hooted. "You want to run for mayor?" He snickered again and wiped his eyes.

Di sat up and backhanded his arm. "What's so funny? You don't think I'm capable?"

"It's not that." He still looked amused. "You've never shown any interest in holding a public office. You don't know the first thing about running a town."

"I can learn. Or am I only a cleaning woman to you, too?"

His smile faded. "Where'd that come from?" Shadows gathered on his face as he studied her. "I've never seen you as less than capable, Diamond. Are you serious about this?"

"Why not?"

"For one thing," he leaned toward her and ran his hand down her arm, "do you want the pressure of running the city *and* a business *and* being mom to an active teenager?

Campaigning by itself is a lot of exhausting work." He took her hands in his. "Honey, I know you could do it if you put your mind to it, but I've never known you to have any aspirations of that sort."

He tried to pull her close again. When she resisted, he said, "Maybe you should first try for a position on city council. Run to represent Eva's district. You'll accomplish more that way than being mayor."

That made sense, but his mocking laughter still rang in her ears. She moved to her side of the bed, punched her pillow, and pulled the covers up, her back to him.

"I'll think about it."

3

City council or mayor?

Di contemplated the question while driving through a light fog the next morning on her way to the car dealership. Did she really want to get into public office? Deal with local politics? Wasn't running a business enough of a challenge?

Clutching the file of paperwork Mitch had forgotten at home, she headed inside and found him in the showroom with a customer. She stepped aside to wait until he finished. An aroma of coffee sifted through the air as a woman approached her with a steaming mug. Her name tag, and her cup, read Liza.

"You must be Mitch's wife," she said. "He mentioned you'd be coming by. I can make sure he gets that, so you don't have to wait around." She took the packet from Di's hand, stuffed it under her arm, and walked over to chat with another salesman.

Di hesitated. Liza's impersonal boldness touched a nerve, tempting Di to snatch the packet back and insist on handing it off herself. But best not to make waves among Mitch's coworkers and trust Liza's promise to get it to Mitch. Swallowing her annoyance, she threw a quick glance at Mitch and his customer on the way out. He broke from the customer just long enough to wink and give her a quick smile.

A stop at the grocery store for that one item she'd forgotten took longer than expected. The tiered racks of personal shoppers clogged the aisles, but she managed to squeeze between them to the jars of salsa. Another woman stopped beside her with a toddler squirming in her cart.

"Aren't you Julianna's mom?" The woman opened a box of fruit gummies and handed the boy a pouch.

"Yes. I'm sorry. I don't remember your name." She looked vaguely familiar. Di shifted the salsa from one hand to the other.

"We haven't met. I saw you with her at the auditions for the children's theater play. My daughter, Zoey, auditioned but she was so nervous she didn't do very well. Julianna came over and encouraged her to keep trying, not give up. Such a nice young lady."

"Well, thank you."

"She said you clean houses?"

Mitch's wife, Julianna's mom, cleaning lady. When had she become a nameless entity?

"I focus more on personal organizing, but yes, I have a cleaning business. Would you like my card?"

"How much do you charge?" The boy threw his snack bag to the floor and fought to stand up in the seat. The woman wrestled him back down while he screamed in protest.

"Call me when you have a minute, and we can discuss cost." Di rooted in her purse, handed her a card, and used the distraction to make a quick getaway.

The fog had deepened into mist by the time she got home, which didn't help her mood. Still stewing about her non-identity, Di stomped into her office. Schedules, an upcoming staff meeting, and ideas for some community classes suggested by her employees all needed her attention, but her mind refused to cooperate. Di threw her pen onto the desk at the very moment Aunt Glori called from the kitchen.

"Yoo-hoo. Anybody home?"

"I'm back here." Di stood to greet her aunt. Though not a blood relative, Gloria had been Eva's best friend since their college days. And Di's surrogate aunty, the one whose affection and attention often salved her bumpy relationship with Eva.

She swept into the office with a hug for Di. "Whoo! It's wet out there. I have a meeting this morning, but I stopped by to see Eva and thought I'd make a quick visit here too. She's excited you're taking her to lunch tomorrow. I still can't believe she forgot to pay her electric bill."

"She wouldn't have lost it if she'd gotten rid of all that junk."

"She doesn't see it that way." Aunt Glori picked up a file folder from the desk and fanned herself.

"I know." Di turned on the ceiling fan for her. "The same old arguments every time. And more."

"More?"

"Nothing. It's not important."

"Tell me." Hands on hips, Gloria tipped her head like a teacher reprimanding a reluctant student.

Di had seen that posture often during her teenage years when Aunt Glori acted as an impartial sounding board for Di's complaints against parental restrictions.

"Apparently, I've disappointed her with my profession. She'd much rather I flipped houses."

Gloria slapped the file folder onto the desk. "Trust me, dear. She talks about you all the time when you're not around. She's very proud of you."

"She's got a funny way of showing it." Di squared up the folder with the others on her desk. "But she's not the only one. Julianna thinks I'm just a cleaning woman, too."

Gloria raised an eyebrow. "Julianna said that?"

"That's what she told one of the other kids at the auditions. And then Mitch laughed when I brought up the idea of running for mayor of Waco."

A brief cackle erupted before Gloria covered her mouth and went into a coughing fit. She choked out a response. "Why would you want to be mayor of Waco? Or anywhere else for that matter."

"Because who am I?" She ticked them off on her fingers. "I'm Eva's daughter, Julianna's mom, Mitch's wife, the cleaning lady, the organizer of junk people can't throw away on their own. I'm tired of being in everyone else's shadow." Di sank into her chair.

Gloria took Di's hands in hers and leaned down to look into her eyes. "Diamond, where is this coming from? Wife, mother, daughter, friend—they're all respectable titles, even without business owner."

Di shook her head and pulled her hands away. "I want a name, my name. I want to be known as Diamond Lange." She raked her fingers through her hair, then hugged her shoulders and hung her head. "Sorry. I didn't mean for all that to spill out."

"I'm glad it did. I had no idea you felt that way."

Di got up and paced around the desk, then turned toward Gloria. "That's not my only reason to run for mayor. Did you know there are plans to demolish Eva's neighborhood and build fancy new homes?"

Gloria frowned. "I'd heard rumors. Did Eva tell you that?"

"No, it came from one of Mitch's co-workers. Mitch said

running for the council seat in Eva's district might be more effective in trying to stop it."

"He's right, although by the time the election rolls around, it could be too late."

Di sat on the edge of her desk and sighed. "You're right. Honestly, the city council doesn't interest me in the least. Neither does being mayor. I have no intention of doing either. I only wanted them so that ..."

Aunt Glori filled in the blank. "... so you'd be known for who you are."

Di pressed her lips together and stared at the floor. Hearing it out loud made it sound selfish.

Aunt Glori pulled her chin up. "There's nothing wrong with being known for what we do. I doubt many remember my name. They only know I'm that real estate agent. The people who know your name are the ones who recognize your worth. Don't waste time fretting about the others."

Di's jaw tightened. "But that's just it. I'm not sure the people who know my name even consider my worth."

"You can't see it right now, but I assure you they do. You've accomplished more than most people have with your business and you have every right to hold your head high."

Gloria glanced at her watch. "Gotta run. Enjoy your lunch with Eva tomorrow and give my love to Julianna and Mitch. We can talk again later if you want." She waggled her fingers at Di and left the office. Her footsteps echoed down the hall, then returned, and she peeked into the office.

"Forgot to mention. I recommended you to a fellow agent. Expect a call from Jill Morgan." Gloria waved again and made her exit.

Her advice didn't entirely quell Di's resentment, but her encouragement dulled the sting. It was a shame the woman never had children of her own. But then Di might not have been able to count on Aunt Glori's listening ear and down-to-earth counsel.

An incoming call brought Di back to her desk chair.

"Diamond Cleaning and Organizing. How can I help you?"

"Di? This is Jill Morgan. Gloria Fuller recommended you."

"Yes, she was just here and told me to expect your call." Di picked up a pen and held it poised over a notepad.

"Great. I have a client who's moving here for work. He's finishing up another project and asked if I could find someone to set up and organize his condo. He wants it ready when he gets here. Gloria said you're the one to do this."

"Absolutely. How soon do you expect him?"

"Next week. He shipped his belongings here and they're due to arrive Monday. Can someone meet me when they get here so I can hand off the key?"

"I'll be there myself. Just let me know what time."

A shiver of excitement ran through Di at the end of the call. Nothing satisfied her as much as organizing. Setting up a whole apartment from scratch was a gift from heaven. She'd have to thank Aunt Glori for the recommendation.

With the affirmation of her work and the addition of a new client, she made good progress on the agenda for her staff meeting. The monthly get-togethers with her cleaning employees, eleven of them, promoted a sense of team cooperation and gave her a chance to learn of any problems or new ideas. A couple of the women had suggested offering classes that might interest her clients—home organization, keeping children's toys under control, or a system for keeping track of important papers. Another asked if they might bring a handyman on staff to tackle all those little maintenance tasks clients asked about.

Di was deep into ideas, scribbling them on her notepad,

when the phone rang. She picked it up without glancing at the caller's number. A woman's high-pitched voice spoke in a rush.

"I need to speak with Diamond, please. It's an emergency."

"This is Diamond." She frowned at the screen that showed Eva's number. This was definitely not Eva.

"Miss Diamond, something's wrong with your mother. You need to come right away."

"Who is this?"

"Lyndee Rae. I'm her cleaning lady."

A spam call, using Eva's phone number.

Di's voice hardened. "My mother doesn't have a cleaning lady. If you've seen her house, you'd know that. Can't you find something better to do than make prank calls?"

"This isn't a prank. Don't hang up. Please." She sounded desperate. "I got here minutes ago and found Miss Eva slumped over the side of her chair. I can't wake her up."

Di hesitated. If this was a hoax, the woman was a good actress. "How do I know you're telling me the truth?"

"Lyin's a sin, ma'am. Please, hurry. I called 911 and they're sending an ambulance."

"911?"

"Yes, ma'am. She's breathing but her pulse is weak. You need to come quick." She paused, then exhaled what sounded like relief. "A siren. Thank you, Lord. Hurry, Miss Diamond. Your mama needs you."

4

The line went dead. Was this real? Di's trembling finger punched in Eva's number. It rang seven times before going to voice mail. If this woman was with Eva, why didn't she answer her phone?

Maybe she'd gone outside to meet the ambulance—assuming this wasn't some sort of con game. Either way, she should check on Eva. If it turned out to be harmless, they could go for lunch today instead of tomorrow. And if it wasn't? She'd find that Linda Whatever-her-name-was and . . . well, she'd figure that out once she knew the situation. Di grabbed her purse, locked the doors, and pushed the speed limit over to Eva's house.

The wet streets didn't help. Her windshield wipers pulsed as she thought over the conversation.

Your mama needs you.

If Eva were conscious, she'd have thrown a royal hissy fit at being called mama. She'd always insisted the term 'mother' made her feel old. Did her resistance to that affectionate title play a part in the barrier that always seemed to stand between them? Was it hard to think of her as a mother when she refused to be called that?

Di turned onto Eva's street and slammed on the brakes. Her heart nearly stopped at the red and blue lights swirling atop a firetruck, an ambulance, and two police cars. Paramedics were wheeling a gurney out the front door. Di threw the car into park and ran to Eva's side.

Straps secured her to the gurney. A sheet over her body didn't hide the EKG leads on her chest. An oxygen mask covered her mouth and nose, and her skin had a pasty look. Di covered Eva's hand with hers, warming it. An oximeter on her index finger measured her pulse.

"Mother! Eva!"

No response, not even a twitch of an eyelid.

"You're her daughter?" asked one of the medics pushing the gurney.

"Yes. What happened? What's wrong?"

"Pulse and breathing are weak. Any health issues we need to be aware of?" Another medic opened the rear doors of the ambulance.

"High blood pressure, arthritis. She had a checkup last month." Di let go as they loaded Eva into the ambulance.

"Who's her doctor?" The medic entered the information she gave him into a tablet, then instructed her to follow them to the hospital.

Di brushed damp bangs from her eyes and started for her car. She glanced toward the house. Two officers walked to their patrol cars and firefighters exited the house with a trauma bag and AED backpack. Behind them, a woman appeared wearing faded jeans and a T-shirt screen-printed with a flowery design. She stopped in Eva's open doorway, her hands clasped in front of her as if in prayer.

"Linda?" Di called.

Her head jerked up. Seeing her, the woman stepped toward Di.

"Lyndee. It's Lyndee Rae. I'm so sorry—"

"Never mind that now. Can you come with me?"

The woman disappeared inside the house, emerging a moment later with two purses, one of them Eva's. She locked the door and dashed to Di's car, tossing Eva's purse inside as she slid into the passenger seat.

"You'll need that." She secured the seat belt.

Di sped to catch up with the ambulance and stayed close behind, taking advantage of the traffic-clearing siren.

The woman clutched the armrest as they merged onto a rainy I-35. "I'm sorry we had to meet under these circumstances, Miss Diamond. Eva talks about you all the time."

"Call me Di." She took her gaze off the ambulance long enough to notice the woman's girl-next-door appeal. If she wore any make-up, it was minimal. Gathered in a low ponytail, her honey-colored hair draped over her shoulder. Di guessed her to be about ten years younger than herself, which would put her in her early thirties. And what did she call herself?

"Say your name again?"

"Lyndee Rae."

Her accent was definitely East Texas, more Southern than the drawl common to other parts of the state.

"You said you're Mother's cleaning lady. Since when?"

"A couple of weeks." Lyndee Rae looked out the side window and exhaled a heavy breath. "Can't say I've accomplished much."

"Trust me, that's not your fault. Tell me what happened this morning." Di switched lanes and sped around a car that pulled in between her and the ambulance. She clenched her jaw, and some unkind words passed through her mind. Can't they tell she's trying to stay with the EMS?

"I was running late," Lyndee Rae said. "Had to wait until my husband could watch our daughter. He mostly works from home. Anyway, I rang Miss Eva's doorbell and knocked but she didn't yell to come in like she usually does. I peeked in the window and saw her slumped over the side of her chair. You know, the one she always sits in?"

Her voice rose in pitch, and she pulled a tissue out of her purse.

"I'd warned her about the dangers of not locking her door, but I'm glad she didn't listen. I was able to let myself in . . . tried to wake her . . . she was still warm and had a pulse, so I called 911 right away. But it took me a minute to remember the name of your company. I found it online." She dabbed at her eyes. "If only I'd been on time—"

Di forced aside the fact that Eva had hired someone else behind her back. "If it's any comfort, my aunt visited her earlier this morning and didn't notice anything wrong. We're lucky you found her at all." She followed the ambulance up to the emergency driveway, then trolled the parking lot for an opening.

"You think it was luck?"

"Good fortune. God smiling on us. Something like that." Di pulled into a parking space and grabbed Eva's purse with her own before getting out.

Lyndee Rae hesitated, then stepped from the car.

"Are you sure you want me here? I hate leavin' you by yourself, but I don't want to intrude. You don't hardly know me."

Di motioned her to come along, and she quick-stepped to catch up. "Any time you want some privacy, just say so. I'll call my husband to come get me."

Di led the way into the emergency waiting area and checked in. She shifted from one foot to the other, waiting for the receptionist to stop tapping keys and staring at her computer screen.

"Okay, it looks like they've got access to your mother's records, but someone will be here to confirm everything with you."

"I'll wait for you out here." Lyndee Rae pointed to some chairs in a corner of the waiting room.

Di was ushered into a small admissions area where she answered questions about Eva's health history, medications, and any recent developments. When she finished, the nursing assistant took her back to the waiting room.

"They'll call you back to your mother's room after they've gotten her settled and she's stable."

In a daze, Di took the seat next to Lyndee Rae. She called Mitch, left a message, then called Gloria.

"I'm at the hospital with Eva. She was brought in unconscious."

Gloria sucked in a breath. "Oh, Lord, no. I'm on my way."

Di slid her phone into her purse and sank back against the chair. She stared unseeing at the terrazzo floor, waiting for her mind to catch up with all that had happened.

"Can I get you something to drink?" Lyndee Rae asked. "A snack maybe?"

Di eyed the vending machines. "Not right now, thanks."

The automatic outside doors whooshed open, and Di jumped up. It was a man in a wheelchair. Too soon for Mitch or Aunt Glori.

Lyndee Rae touched her arm. "Try and relax. They'll probably send Eva for tests, maybe a CT scan. We'll be here awhile."

Di studied her and sank back into her chair. "Sounds like the voice of experience."

"My baby girl is on the list for a heart transplant."

Di stared wide-eyed. "How old?"

"She'll turn five in a couple of months. It's a birth defect. Doctors didn't think she'd make it this long."

"No wonder you weren't eager to come in here. I can't imagine living with that kind of uncertainty." Di met her gaze and held it until she looked away.

Lyndee Rae shrugged. "You do what you have to and thank the Lord for every day she's alive. But I know what it's like to have a medical emergency with someone you love. I just wanted to be sure you were okay with having a stranger beside you."

Orange-scented disinfectant tickled Di's nose as a housekeeping employee worked her way around the room. Ordinarily, she'd watch and evaluate, but at the moment she couldn't care less. Instead, Di shifted her chair toward Lyndee Rae.

"When my mother hired you, what exactly did she ask you to do?"

"She said she wanted someone to clean for her. I figured it'd be vacuuming, dusting, mopping. The usual. But the first time I walked in, I almost turned around and left. Then when she told me her daughter was a professional . . ." Lyndee Rae's hands twisted the strap of her purse. "I hope you don't hold anything against me."

Di's mouth pulled to the side. "I admit I was put off when you said you were her cleaning lady. Every time I offered to help, we ended up arguing."

"She can't admit it's a mess. I think offers to help feel like judgment. Sometimes it's easier to turn to strangers. Who cares what they think? We'll never see them again."

"Did she let you do anything?"

"Not much. Honestly, I think she wants someone to talk to more than she wants a clean house."

Of course. Eva thrived on people interaction. While teaching at the university she'd loved connecting with her students even more than her art. Lyndee Rae understood that need after only a few hours with her.

Di's eyes stung with unshed tears. She'd been too focused on the mess to see Eva's loneliness.

Aunt Glori bustled through the sliding doors at the same time Di's name was called. They both hurried to the examining rooms entrance. The nurse spoke in a hushed voice.

"Just wanted you to know we're taking Eva for a CT scan."

"Can we go along?" Di asked. She slid her arm around Aunt Glori.

"Yes, but you'd have to wait in the hall."

Di glanced back at the outside entry. No sign of Mitch. If they went with Eva, he'd wonder where they were.

"Will they bring her back here?"

"It's possible they might send her up to ICU, in which case we'd let you know. But most likely, she'll come back here."

Where was Mitch? She needed him.

"I'll wait here. Thank you." Di guided Aunt Glori to where Lyndee Rae waited and introduced them.

"I don't understand it." Gloria sniffed. "She seemed fine when I stopped early this morning."

Thirty minutes later, Mitch finally arrived. Di rushed into his embrace. She repeated the explanation of Lyndee Rae finding Eva. "Last we heard, they took her for a CT scan, but it seems they should be back by now."

Lyndee Rae stood to make room for Mitch and excused herself. "You don't need me anymore now that your family's here."

Di reached for her hand and squeezed it in both of hers. "Thank you so much for calling and for staying with me."

"Of course. Please let me know—"

"I will. Put my number in your cell phone and send a text so I'll have your number."

At last, Di was beckoned to the back, but instead of going to Eva's room, she and Mitch and Aunt Glori were ushered into a small consultation room. A doctor entered, closed the door, and pulled a chair around.

Di's stomach clenched at the seriousness of his expression. She reached for Mitch's hand and held tight as the doctor avoided eye contact, leaned his elbows on his knees, and rubbed his palms together. In a firm but subdued voice, he introduced himself and confirmed Di's relationship to Eva, as well as Mitch and Gloria. He settled an intense gaze on Di.

"Your mother suffered a massive stroke this morning. Unfortunately, she never regained consciousness, and—I'm sorry, she died before we could get her back from the CT scan."

Di expelled the breath she'd been holding, then struggled to draw in oxygen. His announcement had sucked the air out of the room.

How is this possible? The woman who is always so full of life is dead?

Gloria put her hand to her mouth and moaned, then reached for Di. Mitch wrapped his arms around both of their shoulders.

Di clasped his fingers and forced a question past the parched desert in her throat.

"Any chance she … might've lived … if … she'd gotten here sooner?"

"Not likely with an event this extreme. When she was admitted, her EEG showed no activity in the brain. The CT scan indicated a large clot. We did everything we could but if she'd survived, her quality of life would've been severely limited. To be honest, it's a wonder she didn't succumb immediately."

He waited several moments, his gaze sliding from Di to Mitch to Gloria and back again. "Again, I'm very sorry for your loss. We'll let you in to say your goodbyes as soon as we get all the equipment moved out of the room. Any other questions?"

Di shivered. Had the room grown colder? Even her brain felt frozen, unable to come up with a rational thought, much less a question.

A knock on the door, a gesture at the narrow window, and he stood. "The only other thing we'll need is the name of the funeral home that will handle the arrangements. If you'll follow me, please..."

Di couldn't. Her limbs were too heavy.

Mitch raised her to her feet and nearly carried her to Eva's room.

Di dropped into a chair at her kitchen table and put her head in her hands. They'd missed lunch and it was getting close to suppertime. But who could think of food at a time like this?

Eva was gone. Nothing else mattered.

She switched her buzzing phone to silent and shoved it to the bottom of her purse. Thoughts of the last time she left Eva came at her like mosquitoes hungry for blood. She'd ignored her own vow to avoid arguing. Left without even a good-bye and refused to come inside again. If she'd known... would she have been kinder, more understanding, less judgmental?

Mitch pulled out a chair for Aunt Glori, then placed his hand on Di's back. She raised her head to look at him. His eyes held an unspoken question.

"What is it?" she asked.

"I left some unfinished business at work. Would you mind?"

"Now?" She hated the whine in her voice.

"Only for a couple of hours. I wouldn't leave you, but I figured with Aunt Glori here—"

Too numb to answer, Di dropped her head to her hands again.

"I'll be back." He kissed the top of her head and slipped out the door.

Di rolled her head from side to side. "How can he do that? Go to work as if nothing has happened."

"He's a man. That whole compartmentalizing their emotions thing. Hugh used to do that, too. Sometimes I envied him. Other times I wanted to slap him." Gloria got up, grabbed a box of tissues from the counter, and set it on the table.

Di pressed her trembling lips together. He wasn't abandoning her. He'd left her in the care of Aunt Glori, the woman she looked to for mothering whenever Eva's priorities didn't include her.

"Julianna will be devastated." Di grabbed a tissue and blew her nose. "She and Eva were kindred spirits, both having that creative streak. Made me jealous sometimes, the way they seemed to understand each other. Eva refused to be called mother, but she reveled in Julianna's name for her."

"Grand Eva suited her perfectly." With a sad smile, Aunt Glori pushed her glasses out of the way and dabbed her eyes with a tissue. "How soon will Julianna be home?"

Di checked the kitchen clock. "Any minute now." Aunt Glori's pinched brow, red-rimmed eyes, and mascara-smudged cheeks with tear tracks down to her chin provided a realization that Di must look every bit as dreadful. "We'd better freshen up or she'll know right off that something's wrong. I'd rather try to break it to her as gently as possible." She went to the sink and pressed a cold, moist paper towel to her eyes and cheeks. She turned to Aunt Glori, who was rinsing her face. "How's this look? Any better?"

Gloria patted her face with a dry towel and looked toward a noise on the other side of the door to the garage. "Is that her? If you want time to figure out how to tell her, you'd better put on a smile, dear."

Julianna burst through the door and dropped her backpack on the floor.

"Mom, I got the part! I'm Cinderella." She rose onto her toes and whirled around the table.

Doing her best to appear happy, Di applauded then caught her in a hug. "That's wonderful, Julianna. I'm so proud of you." Di smoothed a stray hair from her daughter's face and hugged her again.

Gloria joined the hug and planted a kiss on the girl's cheek. "Now I can brag that I'm personal friends with an actress. Will I get an autographed program? A backstage pass?"

Julianna laughed. "Absolutely." She twirled around the room again. "I'm so excited. Is Dad home? Oh! I have to call Grand Eva. She'll be so excited."

Di caught her as she dashed toward her backpack.

"Before you call Grand Eva, I need to tell you something." Di glanced at Gloria, who turned away and grabbed another tissue.

Julianna reached for her backpack. "Hang on. Let me call her. It'll only take a minute. She wanted me to let her know—" Julianna stopped, did a double-take at Di, then Aunt Glori. Her smile disappeared. "Y'all look like you've been crying. What's wrong?"

Di licked her dry lips and put her hands on Julianna's shoulders. "Sweetheart, you can't call Grand Eva. She suffered a severe stroke this morning and she's"—Di swallowed hard, then forced out the last word in a whisper—"gone."

5

"Not Grand Eva." Julianna's incredulous gaze shifted from Di to Aunt Glori and back to Di. A moment of stunned silence ended with a wail. "No-o-o-o!"

Di caught her as she nearly collapsed and guided her into a chair at the table. Her tears brought a fresh flood to Di's eyes.

Julianna stuttered through her sobs. "Wha-what ha— happened?"

Di explained about getting the phone call, the wait at the hospital, and the doctor's distressing news.

"She'll never see me as Cinderella."

Aunt Glori dabbed her eyes. "Well now, you never know. She might have the best seat in the house."

The idea of Eva watching her only grandchild from the heavens warmed Di's heart. She filled the tea kettle and set it on the stove. Coffee would've been preferable, but it was too late in the day.

Julianna wiped the tears from her cheeks and chewed her lower lip for several moments. "When is the funeral?"

"That's something we'll have to decide."

Gloria frowned. "Eva hated funerals." She raised her hand as if holding a cup to alert Di she'd like some tea, too.

"It'll be a memorial since she chose cremation." Di pulled two cups from the cupboard.

"Same thing. You know as well as I that she didn't want any kind of fanfare at her death."

Di set the cups on the counter and extracted tea bags from another cabinet. "Services are for the living, the friends and family left behind. Lots of people will want an opportunity to pay their last respects."

"You'd go against her final wishes?" There was that teacher's glare again.

Di turned her back and waited for the water to boil, her fingers drumming the edge of the counter near the stove.

Julianna cleared her throat. "What will we do with her ashes?"

"Purchase a columbarium niche." This water was taking forever to boil. Di held her hand over the spout to check the heat.

"That's boring. She'd hate being boxed in like that." Julianna shredded the tissue in her hand into strips. "She loved the university. Why not spread her ashes across the campus? Or sprinkle them on the lawn around the art building."

Di gave up on waiting and poured not-quite-boiling water into the cups. She set one in front of Gloria. "We'd have to get permission."

"Not if we each dropped a little here and a little there at different times. They'd never know. Grand Eva would love it." Julianna swiped another tissue and blew her nose.

Gloria tried the tea and grimaced. "What about the house?"

Di swished her tea bag back and forth. "I can't see keeping it. Especially with the new development going in."

"We can't sell Grand Eva's house." Julianna gathered the torn strips of tissue and crumpled them together. "Rent it out for a couple of years until I graduate. Then I can live there while I'm at the university."

Di's cold fingers curled around the warm cup. "It'll take us that long to clear it out."

Gloria stirred sugar into her tea. "She makes a good point. It would be a nice house for some college students. And it's paid for, so it would be additional income for you and Mitch. Help pay for Julianna's tuition."

Di rolled her eyes. "That's all we need. Some frat boys to move in and it'll end up in worse shape than it is now. Besides, if the rumor is false and that neighborhood isn't up for redevelopment, it's still not the kind of place I'd want Julianna or any other young people staying."

She sighed. "We've got time to decide. I'm not looking forward to sorting through all that junk. That reminds me—"

Di hurried out to the garage and returned with Eva's purse. "Her cleaning lady, the one who called me, had the presence of mind to bring this along when we went to the hospital."

Julianna grabbed the large canvas and leather bag with a bold sunflower design and hugged it to her chest. "Can I have it?"

Aunt Glori cocked an eyebrow at her. "You've never liked carrying a purse. Now you want one that's the size of a suitcase?"

Julianna traced her finger around the sunflower on the side. "Grand Eva kept surprises in here for me. When I was little and needed something to occupy my attention, she'd let me dig through her purse. I got to keep any coins I found in the bottom. Sometimes I'd find a stick of gum or a candy bar, or some little puzzle to work on."

"And one time you found her lipstick." Di smirked. "Bright red lipstick all over your cheeks. She tried so hard to scrub it off before she brought you home."

Julianna chuckled. "She never left that in her purse again." Her smile faded as she stroked the purse. "I'll never see her again." She laid the purse on the table and rested her forehead on it, muffling her sobs.

Aunt Glori embraced her from one side, Di from the other, leaning her head against Julianna's. Her daughter's grief intensified her own.

Di squeezed her eyes shut. Would the day ever come when Eva's absence felt normal? When this bottomless pit would no longer be filled with sorrow? She'd been so much younger, more naive when Dad passed away, though his death was as sudden as Eva's. While she missed him deeply, it wasn't the same as losing her mother.

Eva.

At last, Julianna wiped her face and reached into Eva's purse, bringing out one item at a time. Wallet, keys, tissues, hand sanitizer, a nail file and clipper, a prescription pill bottle, a silver ring with a large turquoise stone. She slipped it onto her forefinger and held it out for examination.

"What do you think, Aunt Glori?"

Gloria shook her head. "You're too young and petite for anything that gaudy."

Julianna admired it a moment then reached into the purse again and pulled out a pair of dark sunglasses with rhinestones decorating the frames. She put them on and peeked over the top, mimicking Grand Eva's throaty voice.

"Bless her heart. She must've been vaccinated with a Victrola needle."

Di and Aunt Glori burst out laughing.

"That was perfect," Aunt Glori hooted.

Di giggled. "Just like her."

Julianna shrugged, pulled off the glasses, and blinked several times. "Wow, she must've been half-blind." She shoved her hand deep inside the purse. The bag bulged here and there as she rummaged through it. When she finally pulled out a fistful of coins, her palm held a dime, three quarters, and seven pennies. Sighing, she closed her fingers over them and deposited them in her pocket.

Next, she brought out a handful of receipts. "Any reason to keep these?"

Di sat beside her and checked each one before crumpling and dropping it into a pile on the table.

Julianna unfolded a half sheet of paper. "What's this? Some kind of list—teal floor vase, vintage necklace, rag doll, piano, star painting. Your name's at the top, Mom."

"Let me see that." Di took it from her and studied it. She tapped the paper against her thumb. "These must be the things I'm supposed to keep. I bet she meant to give it to me when we had lunch."

Gloria reached for the paper and murmured each word as she read it. "She wanted you to keep these?"

"Only to pass them on to others who would treasure them like she did."

Gloria looked confused.

Di continued. "The last time we argued about the junk in her house, she said she knew I'd throw it all away when she was gone. But there were a few things she wanted me to pass on to others who would cherish them."

"Except for the piano maybe, I can't think any of these are worth much." Aunt Glori handed the paper back to Di.

"She didn't say they were. For whatever reason, they were important to her."

"That piano." Aunt Glori rolled her eyes. "Walter was the only one who played. She didn't know the first thing about music. After he died, I don't think she ever even had it tuned. Did you take lessons, Di?"

"Only what Dad tried to teach me. I hated practicing and knew I'd never be as good as he was." She squinted while a memory took shape in her mind. "Now that I think about it, I once saw Eva hugging a Raggedy Ann doll. Around the time Dad died, I walked into her room without knocking. She was crying and seemed embarrassed that I caught her like that."

"You're right." Aunt Glori tapped her arm. "I do remember that doll from our college dorm days. It was a gift from her older sister, Dorothy, I think. Eva called her Dottie and apparently, they were very close until Dottie died. I can't remember what she died from at such a young age, but any time Eva needed comfort, she turned to that doll the way I turn to chocolate."

"Poor Grand Eva." Julianna sniffed. "Did she keep it in a special place, Mom?"

Di shrugged. "I never saw it again, and she never told me where I'd find these things."

"You'd think she'd keep them all together if they were important to her." Gloria set her tea aside.

Di sat at the table and sipped from her cup. "That house. I'll try to get over there and figure out a plan of attack. When are you available?"

Gloria shook her head. "I'm booked up until the weekend."

"That's fine. Gives me time to get a roll-off dumpster over there."

"You can't throw away everything." Julianna twisted in her chair to plead with Di. "I want to help."

"What about play rehearsals?"

"I'll work it out. I mean, after all, I am practicing to be Cinderella, right?" Julianna's smile dimmed. "Besides, I want to find other things of Grand Eva's to remember her by."

"Mm-hmm." Di looked at Gloria. "Scary to think this might be how Eva started. Think it's in the genes?"

Gloria pressed her lips together and lifted her gaze to the ceiling without answering.

6

A week later, Di moved through the apartment she'd spent the last five days setting up. A mixed blessing, as it turned out, giving her something to do in the days following Eva's death, but working alone meant a lot of time to dwell on regrets.

Room by room, she checked everything over. The tenant was expected the next day. A fingerprint on the protective glass of a wall hanging caught her attention. Di whisked out her rag to wipe it away, then adjusted it a fraction of an inch. Otherwise, the place looked spotless after one of her ladies had cleaned yesterday, removing the dust and residue from unpacking boxes and setting up furniture. The client should have nothing to complain about when he arrived.

A few books, primarily biographies on historical, political, and sports figures, stood upright on the bookshelf. Architectural journals hinted at his occupation and explained the other photos on the walls showing various types of buildings, including a San Antonio Riverwalk hotel, all lit up at night. But there were no exotic vacation photos. No cute kids or pets. Not even a wife or girlfriend. Nothing of a personal nature. Was he single? Divorced? Or did he move around too much to worry about things like that?

She packed up the few supplies she'd brought and put the key in her pocket to drop off with the real estate agent on her way home. A metallic rasping sound at the door told her she might not have to make that stop. Jill must have decided to make a final inspection herself.

"Hang on, I'm coming." She hurried to the door, but it swung open to reveal a man in cowboy hat, brass buckle at his waist, and cowboy boots below his pressed jeans.

His raised eyebrows mirrored Di's surprise.

She planted herself in the doorway, blocking his entrance. "You're not Jill. Who are you?"

One of his hands gripped the handle of a large suitcase while the other held a garment bag over his shoulder. His mustache and neatly trimmed beard didn't hide his smirk. "I'm the new tenant. And who, may I ask, are you?"

Di sucked in a breath.

That smirk. The voice. Surely not . . .

"We—we weren't expecting you until tomorrow."

"Well, here I am anyway. May I?" He motioned for her to move aside and squeezed past her into the entryway.

She caught a whiff of his fresh, soapy scent as he passed. Her hand went to the diamond at her neck.

He glanced at her. "I assume you're the cleaning lady Jill hired?"

The cleaning lady. He didn't recognize her.

She forced her hand down to her side. "Y-yes, making sure everything was ready for you."

He halted mid-step and turned toward her, tilting his head

to one side. His gaze took in her necklace, then rose to study her face.

"Diamond? Diamond Malone?"

Her cheeks warmed. "Used to be Malone. Now it's Lange. How are you, Scott?" She held out a tentative hand to shake.

He draped the garment bag over a chair and his hand closed around hers. He looked at her just the way he used to, like she was the most fascinating thing alive. She still found it hard to breathe.

He pressed her hand in both of his. "My goodness. It's been a long time."

She pulled away, her fingers reluctant to leave his warmth. "Yes, it has. What are you doing back here in Waco? Jill said you're here for work, but what do you do?"

"Construction. My company's starting a project here. Do you have a minute to sit and talk?" He nodded toward the living room.

Di shouldered her bag of supplies and stepped back, glancing out the door to the hallway. "You'll need to get unpacked and settled in." She started to leave, then turned back and handed him her key. "Don't want to forget that."

He took the key and followed her into the hall. "Thanks. Would you care to grab lunch one day? Reminisce about the old days? Catch up on the last twenty years?"

Di backed a few steps away. "Maybe. Some day when you're free. Jill has my number." She waved and headed for the elevator.

He called after her. "Hey, thanks for setting up the apartment."

She waved again, turned the corner, and punched the button for the elevator, then dropped her forehead against the wall. She drew in and released a long, slow breath.

Scott Jones. Her first love, the one she'd never completely gotten over. She'd dreamed of his handsome features, his polite manners, his attentiveness whenever they were together. None of the other boys she dated had treated her as well as Scott had. How many times since high school had she imagined renewing their romance? She'd fantasized about circumstances bringing them back together after years apart, both free to pursue a more permanent relationship.

But she wasn't free, and this was no fantasy. She would not betray Mitch or damage their marriage. He may not lavish her with attention when she needed it, but he was still a loving husband and a good father to Julianna. Scott showing up now was not the fulfillment of her girlish dreams, but merely a silly coincidence. She pushed away from the wall.

Still, of all people—Scott Jones.

Saturday morning, Di paused at the door to Eva's house. She'd avoided coming here ever since the paramedics had rolled Mother out on the gurney. But she couldn't put it off any longer. Maybe it was best that Julianna and Aunt Glori couldn't make it until later, giving her time to process it all in private. She turned the key and sucked in some fresh air before twisting the knob.

She could do this.

Inside, only Eva's recliner remained free of the clutter and debris that clogged the rest of the living room. Di dropped the boxes of trash bags and latex gloves she'd brought for cleaning.

Trembling, she stumbled to Eva's chair. Her heart ached as she ran her hand over the arm where Lyndee Rae had found Eva unconscious. Di sank onto the seat, inhaled the lingering medicinal scent mixed with a faint, floral hint of her mother's perfume.

Closing her eyes to the mess around her, she recalled better times before arguments over the clutter had become the norm. Her emergency appendectomy in junior high when Eva spent the night dozing in a chair in her hospital room. Had she ever thanked her for that? Helping Eva decorate for the high school prom. The two of them shopping for her wedding dress. When had she become so critical of Eva? When had she assumed the parent role and reduced Eva to that of a stubborn child?

Di gave in and let her tears wash over her guilt and regrets, thankful at least for the box of tissues Eva kept on the floor beside her recliner. She gave herself five minutes, then dried her face and took a deep breath. She could do this. She had to.

But where to start? If it weren't for her promise to Eva, she'd be tempted to light a match and let it all burn. Were the items on that list worth the effort? Searching for them would be akin to finding five needles in the proverbial haystack. Four, actually. The piano was right there in plain sight, currently holding six knickknacks and a couple of vases with silk flowers. Neither of the vases were of a teal color.

Rising, Di picked up a pink spring jacket left atop a stack of books on the piano bench. She held it up. Too small to fit Eva. Julianna's? Or maybe a visitor had left it. She draped it across the back of the recliner and moved the books onto the floor. White rings, likely left by Eva's coffee cups, marred the piano's bench, and when she lifted the lid, she found old music books and sheet music inside, likely untouched in—how many? Twenty years.

Hands on hips, she surveyed the living room. Normally, she'd pull everything out onto the floor to be sorted and put away, but the floor was part of the problem. It needed clearing first. She shook out a garbage bag and slipped a pair of gloves over her hands. No telling what kind of germs might be lurking in this house. To be fair, Eva did try to keep the house clean, if not neat, until her health became a problem. She could be downright nitpicky at times, fussing over a tiny spot of grease Di missed when washing a pan but completely blind to the mess all around her.

She gathered the newspapers scattered next to Eva's recliner and stuffed them into her trash bag. Moving methodically around the room, she picked up handfuls of bulk mailings, receipts, and other miscellaneous papers and shoved them into the bag. Later, she'd empty it into Eva's recycling bin.

An hour passed while she sorted some of the mess into various piles about the room—books here, clothing there, knickknacks beyond, and anything that didn't fit those categories landed on the couch. She picked up the vases from the piano, sneezed from the dusty flowers, and set them back in place. She'd deal with them later.

The doorbell rang, followed by a knock. Di checked the time. Too early for Julianna, and Aunt Glori would've announced her name. She'd locked the door when she came in, but at least there was now a clear path to the entrance. Something crunched under her foot. Well, almost clear.

"Who is it?" She peeked through the window.

"Lyndee Rae. I think I left my jacket here."

Di opened the door and waved her hand toward the mess.

"Come in if you dare."

Lyndee Rae entered, her gaze sweeping over the chaos.

"I'm so sorry about Eva. I didn't see anything about a funeral, or I might've come. I didn't know if I should, seeing's how I only knew her for a week. But then my little girl got sick and—"

"Don't worry. I'm sorry about your daughter. I hope she's

okay." Di stepped over the pile of books and lifted the jacket from the recliner. "This must be yours."

"Yes, that's it. Thanks." Lyndee Rae hung the jacket over her arm. "I've been by a few times hoping to catch someone here so I could pick it up. When I saw your car, I decided to stop." She looked around the room again. "You've made some progress. Are you here all by yourself?"

"My daughter and Aunt Glori had planned to be here but other commitments kept them away." She looked about the room and let go of a sigh.

"Would you like me to help? My husband took our daughter for a date this morning, so I've got time."

"Oh, you don't want to spend your free time this way. Go do something fun, like a movie or shopping. Maybe a mani-pedi."

Lyndee Rae smiled. "Honestly, none of those appeal to me. And we're trying to save as much money as we can right now, so—" She shrugged. "This doesn't cost anything. Besides, I'd love some grown-up female conversation for a change."

"How is your daughter? What's her name?"

Lyndee Rae's face clouded. "Paisley. I'm not sure how much longer she can survive. We're praying a heart becomes available soon, but of course, that means someone else will lose their child." She blinked and rubbed at the corner of her eye.

"That's a tough spot to be in." Di paused. "Hey, if you've nothing better to do, I'd love the company. Grab a bag and some gloves." She explained her strategy.

Lyndee Rae suggested she could concentrate on clearing the table in the open concept dining area. "You'll need to sort photos and paperwork and other things. And you'll have a place to eat lunch or take a break."

"Good thinking. I thought I was the professional here." Di grinned, then grimaced as she held up a crusty bowl with mold clinging to the spoon. "If you find any more like this, throw it out."

Lyndee Rae rubbed a wash rag over the table's uncluttered surface. "I hate to leave you, but it's almost lunchtime, and Kurt and Paisley should be home soon." She rinsed the rag in the sink, wrung it out, and hung it over the faucet.

Di looked up. Not only was the table clean, but the chairs surrounding it were free of clutter as well. Bulging trash bags rested at one corner. Lyndee Rae returned to the table and pointed to a large mixing bowl in the middle.

"Anything I wasn't sure whether to keep, I put in that bowl. I figured you can sort through it all later."

Di brushed a hair from her face with her forearm. "You've been a big help. Having someone to talk to made the time pass quickly, and you obviously have some cleaning and organizing talents of your own."

"I've been doing some housecleaning jobs whenever Kurt is free to watch Paisley. Every little bit helps."

"I hope a donor comes through for you real soon." Di scanned the room. They'd only begun. So much yet to do with two bathrooms, Eva's bedroom, two smaller bedrooms, the closets, the kitchen, and the garage. She studied Lyndee Rae as she retrieved her jacket and headed for the door. "Could I interest you in a steady job?"

Lyndee Rae stopped, her hand on the doorknob. "I can't be very dependable with Paisley's condition."

"Work when you can, right here. Bring your daughter with you if you're comfortable with that. Just record your hours." Di named an hourly rate of pay.

"That's very kind, but please don't feel sorry for me."

"I'm not offering because I feel sorry for you. You handled Eva's stroke, and I've seen you work. I need help with this house, and I think you're the one who can do it."

"That would be an answer to prayer." Lyndee Rae's eyes shimmered. "I'll talk to Kurt, but I think the answer will be yes."

7

"Where's Julianna this fine Saturday night?" Mitch slouched in his favorite armchair, a glass of sweet tea in hand, his stockinged feet propped on the coffee table.

"Namiko was taking her to a movie and then over to a friend's house." Di wrinkled her nose at the faint foot odor and frowned at a hole in the heel of his sock. Did anyone darn socks anymore? Replacing this button on his shirt was about the extent of her sewing talents.

"Does Prince Charming know Cinderella has to be home by midnight?" Mitch sipped his sweet tea.

"He does. Hasn't missed a curfew yet, which is more than I can say for the last boy she dated."

A hint of a smile touched Di's lips as memories of Scott Jones came to mind. She'd been grounded more than a few times for sneaking in past midnight. Being a couple years older, he'd enjoyed a bit more freedom when they were dating.

Her hand stilled from pulling a threaded needle through the button, and her gaze swept Mitch's long figure, still strong and trim in his mid-forties. For a moment, she imagined Scott in his place, then shook the image from her mind. Should she mention him to Mitch? No reason to, really. With Scott working construction, their paths weren't likely to cross. She'd purposely made him go through Jill to contact her, doubting he'd go to the trouble. Isn't *Let's get together* the expected thing to say when reconnecting with an old friend? How often does anyone follow through?

Mitch surfed the television channels, and Di heeded her internal warning to change the channel playing in her mind.

"We've only got a couple more years left before Julianna starts college. Why don't we go somewhere special for vacation this summer?"

"Where?" Mitch turned off the television, yawned and rested his head back on the chair.

"I'd like the mountains, but Julianna probably prefers the beach. What about you?"

"I could go either way. The two of you can decide but do it soon so I can put in for the time off." He yawned and closed his eyes.

Di jabbed her thumb and winced. That was the third time tonight. After a full day of cleaning out Eva's trash, she was too tired for hand sewing.

Mitch's head lolled to one side, and she touched his arm.

"Why don't you go on to bed?"

His eyes popped open. "I'm okay. Just resting." His eyelids slid shut, but a moment later, he asked, "What were you saying?"

"About what?"

"I thought you were talking about vacation plans."

"We were. You said we could go to Hawaii and explore the mountains and beaches."

He opened one eye and squinted at her. "Nice try."

She grinned. "Just seeing if you're awake."

"I am." He nestled deeper into his chair.

Di finished off the last few stitches. "I offered Lyndee Rae a job today."

"Who's Lyndee Rae?" He mumbled, barely opening his mouth.

"The woman who found Eva Remember? You met her at the hospital. She stopped by the house today and ended up helping me clear out a bunch of stuff. She can't work regular hours but . . ." Di tied a knot and cut the thread. "Makes me sad to think her little girl needs a heart transplant. Must be terrible, never knowing if your child will be alive next year or next week. I only hope I haven't made a mistake. I didn't promise anything beyond helping me with the house. Not sure I'll have enough work to keep her on after that. You think that's okay?"

A loud snore answered her.

She recalled the way Scott greeted her earlier, his attention focused completely on her.

No, don't go there. Early in their twenty-year marriage, Mitch had been as attentive as Scott. Had they become an old married couple so soon? Mitch worked hard to provide for them and was tired after a long week. So was she.

Chasing Scott's image from her mind, she rustled Mitch awake and herded him toward the bedroom, turned off the light, and followed.

———

Lyndee Rae made it clear she wouldn't work on Sundays, but Aunt Glori and Julianna accompanied Di to Eva's house the next afternoon.

Gloria halted inside the door. "I can see the carpet."

Julianna paced around the newly cleared area in the living room. "It looks bigger now."

The sight of Eva's recliner silenced both of them. Gloria turned away and hurried into the kitchen. Julianna fell to her knees in front of it and leaned forward as if resting her head on Eva's lap.

Di's eyes clouded. She laid her hand on Julianna's shoulder which shook with quiet sobs.

Gloria called from the other room. "Diamond, have you cleaned out the fridge yet?" The refrigerator door opened with a slight hiss of suction. "Eeuw. Obviously not. I'll start here."

Di whispered into Julianna's ear. "We don't have to stay in here. Would you rather work with me in Eva's bedroom?"

Julianna swallowed hard and nodded. "Give me a minute."

Di left her and entered the master bedroom. Judging by the clutter on the bed, Eva had been sleeping in her recliner for months. A path wound around the bed to the dresser and the over-crowded closet beyond. Cardboard boxes of various sizes lined the outer edge of the path, all piled atop each other like a life-size Jenga puzzle. Who knew what lay within them?

Di retrieved garbage bags and gloves from the living room and sorted through the debris on the bed. Julianna soon joined her, examining every leaflet, brochure, and flyer before dropping them into the trash bag.

"It'll take forever if you keep stopping to read everything." Di shook the bag to settle the contents.

Julianna shrugged. "I know, but a lot of them are from when Grand Eva was still teaching. Art shows, classes . . . It's interesting." She shuffled through another stack of papers and pulled out an 8x10 photo. "How did this get mixed in with all the other stuff?"

Di caught her breath at the sight of her parents' wedding portrait. "I haven't seen that in years." She took it in hand to study it. Older than most newlyweds when they married in their mid-thirties, her parents still appeared young in the picture. Eva was nearly forty when Di came along.

Julianna leaned against Di's shoulder. "That's Grandpa? I don't remember much about him."

"That's him. You were pretty young when he had his heart attack." How she missed his gentle smile and teasing ways.

"I sort of remember Grandpa being tall, or was I just little?"

"You're right. He stood close to six feet, much taller than Eva. Probably why he's sitting in the picture and she's standing." Di set it safely aside and went back to sorting.

After dropping another stack of papers into the bag, Julianna snatched up a notebook and hugged it to her chest. "This is what I've been looking for." Abandoning her task, she leafed through the stiff pages of Eva's sketchbook.

Di tied the top of the trash bag and carried it out to the kitchen. She scrunched her nose at the odor of sour milk and spoiled meat permeating the air.

Gloria paused from scrubbing the inside of the refrigerator and pointed to another white garbage bag. "I threw everything out. Hold your nose and take that with you. It's double-bagged."

Di tossed the latest additions onto the overflowing garbage bin beside the house. She should've ordered that roll-off dumpster.

Back inside, she sniffed the air. "Smells better already. Thanks for taking care of that."

Gloria stood back from the fridge and wiped her wrist across her forehead. "Any idea who might take that piano off your hands?"

"I thought I'd check with a church or a school. Maybe one of the small private schools that doesn't have a budget for a new piano?"

Gloria rinsed and wrung out her rag in the sink, then stepped into the living room and eyed the old upright. It stood tall and solid, though lacking much ornamentation. Once shiny, the maple veneer now looked dull with scratches here and there and a pockmark or two. Several of the ivories were missing from the keys.

"It's not bad looking, considering its age. Let's see how it sounds." Aunt Glori plunked a few keys and grimaced. "Only Beethoven could put up with that. After he lost his hearing, of course."

"Should I get it tuned before offering it?"

"Pianos are tuned after moving them, but I'm not sure how much good it will do. Wait until you have someone interested." She gave a nod toward the bedroom. "What's next? You need some help in there?"

"Sure." Di led the way. "The bed is mostly done, so boxes, closet, or dresser. Take your pick."

"I'll take the door on the left for fifty dollars." Mimicking an old game show, Gloria picked her way along the path past Julianna and the dresser to the wardrobe. "Good gravy, you couldn't squeeze a sheet of paper into this closet."

Di positioned herself between Gloria and the bed. "There's enough room to sort them here. Pass them to me." She accepted clusters of apparel and laid them on the bed in piles of tops, dresses, pants, and skirts.

Holding the sketchbook in front of her face, Julianna backed away. "What's that smell? Is it coming from the clothes?"

"Eau de moth ball." Gloria transferred another batch of clothes to Di.

Julianna backed farther. "Moth ball?"

"They were used to keep moths from eating woolen

sweaters and garments. Smells as bad as the kitchen did." Di laid an evening dress of blue satin on the bed.

Julianna wrinkled her nose but stepped forward and spread the skirt. "Grand Eva wore this? It's so elegant."

"In her younger days. Probably for some celebrity art reception. Too bad we weren't the same size." Gloria held up another dress and studied it, her mouth pulling to one side. "I doubt these would be of any use, even for a clothing charity. They're mostly out of style. Maybe a school theater department would be interested."

Di shrugged. "They'd probably have someone who can alter them. I wonder how many plays are set in the '60s and '70s."

Julianna set aside her sketchbook and the three worked until the last of the hanging clothes were deposited on the bed.

Gloria poked her head inside the closet. "That's it except for the shoes and other stuff in here. Oh, look at this." Without the clothes to muffle the sound, a slight echo followed her voice. She reached deep inside and brought out a dark green lacquered box. Mother of pearl hummingbirds and flowers outlined in gold decorated the top in Asian style.

"Her jewelry box." Julianna shoved aside the clothes on the bed and patted a spot for Gloria to sit. She climbed on next to her and admired the intricate design. "It's gorgeous. I claim it." At Di's tight-lipped frown, she blushed and added, "I mean, don't get rid of it. If neither of you want it, I'd like to have it. Please."

Gloria opened the box. A partitioned tray held earrings, brooches, and several rings similar to the one Julianna found in her purse.

Di picked up a pair of dangly sapphire earrings. "I remember Daddy giving her these for Christmas one year."

"I bet she wore them with that evening dress." Julianna fingered a sparkling brooch. "Are these real diamonds?"

"I doubt it. Dad didn't make that much money."

Julianna looked at Di. "What about your necklace? Isn't that a real diamond?"

"A graduation gift." Di touched the diamond at the base of her throat. "Diamond is my birthstone and my name. In my younger days, I decided I deserved a diamond necklace. Eva and Dad gave me one with a cubic zirconia when I turned thirteen. But that wasn't good enough for me, so Dad promised me a real stone only if I earned straight A's until I finished high school."

Julianna's eyes opened wide. "And you did?"

Di nodded. "I did."

Aunt Glori clicked her tongue. "Shows what a little motivated determination can do." She eyed the jewelry box. "Ready to see what's in the bottom?" She lifted the tray from the velvet-lined box, revealing several intertwined necklaces.

Drawing a sharp breath, Aunt Glori set the tray on the bed and with trembling fingers worked to untangle the necklaces. At last, she held up one, her eyes glistening while her hand closed around it.

She held it to her wet cheek. "Oh, Eva."

8

Di exchanged a look of concern with Julianna. She wrapped her arm around Gloria's shoulders. "Aunt Glori? What—"

Gloria inhaled and let her breath out slowly. She pressed her fingers to her eyes, then laid the gold necklace on her lap, spreading out the sides that bore rhinestones clustered around emerald gemstones. A larger teardrop gem surrounded by more sparkling rhinestones hung from the center.

"I used to shop antique stores for vintage jewelry. This was my favorite find. I fell in love with it the moment I saw it." Gloria sniffed and pulled a tissue from her pocket before continuing. "I showed it to Eva, and she begged to wear it for one of her fancy art events. I agreed, expecting to get it back after the event. But then we had a silly falling-out. She claimed she lost it, that the clasp broke, and the necklace fell off without her realizing it."

Julianna shifted beside her. "You never got it back?"

Gloria shook her head.

"What was she so angry about?"

Gloria took Julianna's hand in hers. "I dated your grandfather, Walter"—she reached for Di's hand as well—"for a couple of years until I met Hugh."

Julianna changed to a sitting position and faced her. "Hugh was your husband?"

"Yes. I knew right away Hugh was the man I wanted to marry. I broke up with Walter, and Eva went after him. I was glad she did. I wanted her to be happy and Walter was a nice guy, just not right for me. But Eva had a stubborn streak even back then. When the two of them argued, Walter would come to me for advice. I was her best friend, after all, and knew her better than anyone. But eventually, Eva got jealous and accused me of trying to hang onto him." Gloria wore a sad smile. "Silly, but when you're young and full of hormones, you often can't see the truth."

Di squeezed her hand. "Did you believe she lost the necklace?"

"No. I always knew she had it."

"Wait." Julianna held up her hand. "She borrowed your favorite necklace, lied about losing it, and refused to give it back to you? Why did you stay friends with her?"

"I almost didn't. We went for months without speaking. Maybe a year, I don't remember. But I missed her. I finally decided I didn't want to lose Eva. Our friendship was worth more to me than any old piece of jewelry."

Di lifted the necklace from Gloria's lap and held it up in front of her. "Is it a painful reminder, or would you like to finally have it back?"

Gloria's eyes glistened. "I'd love to have it back even if it brings back a sad memory."

Di fastened it around her neck. "It's perfect on you."

Julianna gave her a hug. "You look beautiful, Aunt Glori."

Gloria looked down and touched the teardrop stone.

"Sometimes pain teaches us lessons we can't learn any other way, like the worth of a good friend."

―――

Spending Wednesday morning with a client provided a nice break from cleaning out Eva's house. Cora Zimmerman, a widow who'd been married for six decades, had hired Di to help cull her late husband's clothes from her closet.

"He's been gone three years, and I'm finally ready to clean out the old, change things up, and make the house look and feel the way I want," she said. "But we need to do it ASAP before I lose my determination."

They'd worked since early morning, clearing out and organizing Cora's closet the way she wanted it. Including her shoes. The woman had more footwear than a shoe store.

Di's stomach growled when she left Cora's house close to 1:00. That shaky feeling was signaling a drop in her blood sugar. She was famished, but wanted real food, not the drive-thru kind. A sign for Ninfa's restaurant lured her into the parking lot. Perfect—chips and salsa to take the edge off and Mexican food that doesn't require a long wait time.

The lunch crowd was thinning out as a host led Di to a table for two. She placed her order and dipped a salty tortilla chip into the salsa, savoring the tangy crunch.

She planned to spend the rest of the day at Eva's. Lyndee Rae would meet her there this afternoon. With luck, they'd finish clearing the living room. Or maybe she'd ask Lyndee Rae to work there while she went through more boxes in Eva's bedroom.

A familiar voice spoke her name.

"Five stars and one Diamond. This place rates even better than I remember." Scott Jones stood across the table from her, a teasing smile between his mustache and beard. "May I join you?"

Di glanced at the four men with him and swallowed hard. He directed them to sit at another table and waited for her nod before removing his cowboy hat and taking a seat.

Seeing him like this gave her an odd sense of being back in their high school lunchroom with his football buddies nearby. His chambray shirt, tanned face, and dark blond hair, slightly mussed from the hat, set the old familiar butterflies flitting about her stomach. Several gulps of iced tea failed to drown them.

Scott reached for a tortilla chip. "What did you order?"

"Chicken fajitas."

"Sounds perfect." A server set a sizzling plate before her, and he placed an order for the same. "Don't wait for me. Go ahead and eat while it's hot."

Maybe some food would smother the butterflies. Di scooped some chicken onto her tortilla and folded the sides over. "So, you're doing construction? I thought you went to school for a teaching degree."

"I did. Switched to engineering halfway through my sophomore year and ended with a double major in that and construction management." He grabbed a napkin to catch salsa dribbling into his whiskers. "Do you remember me working on that crew the summer after high school graduation?"

"Oh, yes. You were filthy by the end of the day."

He laughed. "Sorry about that. I worked my way through college building houses and liked it a whole lot better than being stuck in a classroom. Maybe it was all those Legos I played with as a kid." He grinned and popped a whole chip into his mouth. "What about you?"

"I put myself through school cleaning houses, majored in

business, and started my own company. These days, I hire ladies to do the dirty work and stick with organizing. That's why Jill called me to set up your apartment."

"Best arrangement I've had so far. I mean that."

His eyes held a certain sparkle, sending the stomach butterflies into motion again.

Get over it, girl. You're not sixteen anymore.

"So, what's your job on this project?" she asked.

"I'm the boss. Jones Construction and Engineering." He thanked the server for bringing his order out.

"It's your company?"

"Yes, ma'am."

"What kind of project are you working on?"

"Some people flip houses. We flip neighborhoods. Buy up old rundown properties, tear 'em down, and replace them with beautiful new homes." He raised a filled tortilla to his mouth.

Di's food caught in her throat. "I've heard there are plans to destroy the Oak Grove subdivision. Is that you?"

"I prefer to call it revitalization." His chewing slowed as he met her gaze. His eyes grew wide. "That's your old neighborhood, isn't it? How could I forget? You don't still live there, do you?"

She shrugged. "I don't, but my mother does. Or she did." Di paused, tipped her head back, and blinked away the tears before they could fall. She would not cry here, not in public, not in front of Scott. "Eva passed away suddenly less than two weeks ago."

Scott leaned back, closed his eyes and hung his head. "I'm sorry to hear that. Miss Eva was one-of-a-kind." He wiped his hand on the cloth napkin and reached across the table to squeeze hers.

No wedding ring. His palm was softer than she'd expect for someone in his line of work. And she shouldn't be noticing such things. She resisted the urge to squeeze back and pulled away.

He leaned forward. "Diamond, I had no idea Eva still lived there. Had she been sick?"

"She wasn't in the best of health, but according to the doctor she suffered a massive stroke. That was completely unexpected."

He winced. "That's a shame. Was moving too much for her?"

Di shook her head to clear the grief. Her throat hurt from holding back tears, but she steadied her voice. "She wasn't moving."

Scott scratched at his temple. "She was supposed to be out by now. We made generous offers on all the houses and sent notices to vacate."

"Eva never mentioned any offer for her house. In fact, she stubbornly refused every suggestion I made about moving to a better neighborhood. If she got a warning notice, it's lost somewhere in the mess."

She paused, debating how much to reveal. "I'm embarrassed to admit Eva was a hoarder, or at least close to becoming one. You can imagine the conflict that caused between us." Rubbing her thumb on the glass of tea, Di tipped her head and mulled over a sudden thought. "Maybe that's why she hired Lyndee Rae."

"Who?"

She looked back at Scott. "Just before she died, she hired a cleaning woman without telling me, a woman named Lyndee Rae. That's who found her unconscious the morning she died."

Scott clasped his hands together, elbows on the table, and gazed at her with an intensity that made her quiver. "I'm so sorry, Diamond. How recent did you say this was?"

"Week before last."

He hung his head. "My timing is awful. I thought we had all the properties cleared."

"Are you really going to level the neighborhood?"

"A block at a time. We're working on getting all the utilities disconnected and checking for hazardous materials that will need special handling. After that, we start bulldozing."

"How long before you get to Eva's block?"

Scott frowned and wiped crumbs from his face. "If I'm correct in remembering where she lived, a couple of weeks. Three at most."

Di stifled a gasp. Three weeks to clear out Eva's house? Impossible.

He went on talking about plans for the neighborhood until they finished their meal. After insisting on paying for hers, Scott walked her out to her car and said goodbye.

She pretended to take a call while he and his men loaded up, but as soon as they exited the parking lot, she dropped her forehead onto the steering wheel and groaned. How could he do this? He wasn't at all concerned about the people he had displaced. It was all simply a business transaction, one he was so excited about he hadn't even given her a chance to ask about his personal life.

Wait until Aunt Glori—

Di grabbed her phone again and speed-dialed Gloria. She relayed the plans for the neighborhood in as much detail as she could recall.

"Honestly, I have mixed feelings about it," she said. "I mean, the neighborhood was going downhill, and it would be nice to see some new homes in there. But taking it all down and starting over? People have invested their lives in that neighborhood. Isn't it wrong to take that away from them?" Di started the engine.

"Some people call it progress." Aunt Glori paused. "Scott

Jones sounds familiar. Isn't that the boy you cried over in high school?"

"You remember that?"

"A nice young man, as I recall. You had it bad for him."

"I did. And I'll admit he still puts my stomach all aflutter but . . ." Di considered how to describe her new impression of him. "I realize I don't really know this 40-something man who owns a construction company and flips neighborhoods."

"Well, that's understandable. A lot of muddy water has passed under that bridge. Think you can clear out the house before he bulldozes it?"

"Only my promise to Eva keeps me from letting him demolish it as is. But if I'm going to keep my word, I'll have to put all my own appointments on hold until we get it cleaned out."

"Or until you find the items on her list. If that's your objective, forget about clearing stuff out. Just work on finding those and let the rest go."

Aunt Glori was right. Cleaning out a house slated for bulldozing made no sense at all. She had the piano and they'd found the vintage necklace. All she had to do was find the remaining items on Eva's list—a doll, a vase, and a star painting. How hard could it be?

9

"How's your new employee working out?" Mitch picked up a stray carrot from the counter and munched on it while Di cleared that evening's supper dishes from the table.

"Lyndee Rae is great. She worked on the living room today, and I emptied Mother's dresser and dug through boxes in her bedroom. So, we've made some progress. It's nice having someone to talk to even though we're in different rooms."

Especially someone who understands grief and isn't afraid of a few tears.

The door from the garage opened and Julianna rushed in from play practice. "Mom, Dad, I've got a great idea for a memorial for Grand Eva. You're going to love it."

Di pointed to the oven. "I kept your dinner warm for you."

Julianna followed her around the kitchen while Di donned an oven mitt, removed the plate from the oven, and set it on the table.

"Listen to this. You know the arts building at the university? We build a garden right there by the main doors. We plant different kinds of sunflowers and mix Grand Eva's ashes in with the dirt. We get students to paint a sunflower mural on the wall behind the garden, so it'll still be pretty when they're out of season." Her eyes shone and her cheeks flushed pink with excitement.

Di and Mitch looked at each other, and Di smiled. "I do love it. That sounds perfect."

"Eva would be thrilled." Mitch high-fived Julianna, who then clapped her hands.

"You really think so?"

Di motioned for her to sit and eat. "My only hesitation is whether the university will allow it. Their staff will have to maintain the garden and they may not appreciate a mural on their building. But it never hurts to ask. The worst they can say is no."

Julianna stared at her plate, her enthusiasm fading. "If they say no, could we do it somewhere else? Like Grand Eva's house maybe?"

Di hesitated. "Maybe." How could she break the news that Eva's house would be rubble in three weeks?

Mitch tugged on Julianna's ponytail. "How was play practice, Cinderella?"

"I need to work on my lines. Dress rehearsal is two weeks from today." She turned to Di. "Mom, I invited Namiko to come over and help with Grand Eva's house on Sunday, if that's okay. He and I could bring stuff down from the attic."

"That's very kind of you both." Di tossed a pod into the dishwasher and pressed the button. A soft whooshing sound added background noise to their conversation. "Mitch, I could really use your help with the garage."

"No problem. Sunday works for me, too." He held up his carrot to make a point. "The family that cleans together . . . gets dirty together. Or something like that." He leaned against the counter and bit off another piece of the carrot with a snap.

"Find anything interesting today, Mom?"

"Baby clothes, toys from my childhood, black-and-white photos—mostly of people I don't know. Blankets—some of them moth eaten—yarn, dried paints and other craft supplies, and lots of old clothing that probably hasn't been worn since Eva and Dad were in college. I can't believe she kept it all."

Julianna got up and filled a glass with water from the faucet. "Nothing from the list?"

"Nope." Di brushed a hair from her forehead.

Mitch took a clean glass from the cupboard and drew some water too. "It'll take months to get rid of all that stuff."

"Well, there's been a change of plans," Di said. "I'm leaving it as is."

He stopped the glass halfway to his mouth. "Why?"

"We have the piano, and the necklace. All we need is to find the other things on Eva's list. A doll, a vase, and a painting."

"But you can't just leave the junk there," Julianna said, "if you're going to rent the house or sell it."

Ready or not, she'd have to break the news now. "That won't be happening. We won't be renting or selling it."

Mitch raised an eyebrow. "We're not?"

Julianna stared at her with a furrowed brow.

Di hung the dishrag over the sink divider and faced them. "Your co-worker was correct, Mitch. Eva's whole neighborhood is slated for redevelopment. The houses have been bought up and will be torn down, replaced with new, probably larger, homes."

Julianna gasped. "Grand Eva's house, too?"

Di nodded. "I'm afraid so."

"They can't do that." She slammed her palm onto the table.

"You're certain? Where'd you hear that?" Mitch asked.

"Straight from the owner of the company that's doing the work. He called it flipping neighborhoods."

"Is he local? Would I know him?"

"I doubt it. He's based in Austin." Di hesitated. "His name is Scott Jones." She grabbed the dishrag again and wiped the counters.

Julianna snagged a cookie from the tin on the table. "How'd you meet him? Was he a client?"

"Not exactly. He grew up here in Waco and we went to school together. A long time ago." She avoided Mitch's gaze. But why? She hadn't done anything wrong. She glanced up as recognition dawned in his eyes.

"Isn't that the guy you were crazy about in high school?"

Julianna sent her a sly grin. "Ooh, Mom, an old boyfriend? Is he still cute?"

Heat rose in Di's cheeks, and she busied herself collecting Julianna's plate and utensils. "He's here to oversee the project. He showed up at the restaurant where I stopped for lunch."

"You had lunch with him?" Julianna's teasing tone wasn't helping. "Can I meet him?"

"He was with his work crew." Di snuck a nervous peek at Mitch but couldn't read his expression. She'd never lied to him before and wasn't really lying now. So why did she feel guilty when she hadn't done anything wrong?

"They're in the final stages before they raze the houses. He said we've got two to three weeks until they get to Eva's. Aunt Glori suggested we look for the items on Eva's list and not worry about cleaning out the junk." She waited for Mitch to comment but he remained silent, even though she could almost see the thoughts whirling in his head.

"That makes sense." Julianna looked for Mitch to agree, but he failed to respond. Her grin evaporated. After shifting her gaze between the two of them, she rose uneasily from the table. "I think I hear my homework calling." She grabbed another cookie and hurried from the room.

Mitch finally lifted his gaze to Di, and she read the question in his eyes.

"That was thirty years ago, Mitch. It's not like I arranged to see him."

"I would hope not. Did you know he was back in town?" He rested his hands on the counter on either side of him and crossed one ankle over the other.

She explained about setting up his apartment and his early arrival.

Mitch asked, "How long were you in the apartment with him?"

"Five minutes, tops. We recognized each other, exchanged pleasantries, and I gave him the extra key I had."

"And your phone number?"

"No!" Di slapped the dishrag onto the counter. "He never asked. I never offered. And that was uncalled for."

Mitch held his palms up. "You're right. I'm sorry. It's just . . . it bothers me that you told Aunt Glori about seeing him but didn't bother to tell me until now."

Di crossed her arms. "I called Aunt Glori because I thought she'd want to know about the real estate development. Mitch, I was sixteen when I dated Scott. Long before I met you."

He came and took her in his arms. "You're right. I'm sorry. Just be careful, okay?"

I'm trying. I really am trying.

———

Three weeks. More like two now that a week had passed since she'd met Scott at lunch.

Morning sunlight poured through the window as Di

scanned the cardboard boxes still to be opened in Eva's bedroom. "A vase, a doll, and a painting." She sighed. "You could've at least told me where to find these things, Mother. But then you probably didn't know either." She wrestled another carton, flimsy with age, from among the jumble and pulled open the flaps. Yearbooks, an old honor cord, photos. Julianna might enjoy sorting through the memorabilia in this box. She set it aside to take home.

The doorbell rang and she rose to answer it. With the deserted look of the neighborhood, she'd been locking the door while here by herself. Peeking through the side window, she saw Lyndee Rae. But when she opened the door, a little girl with a princess backpack entered. Pink bow barrettes pinned her long golden hair back on the sides. An odd bluish tint rimmed her lips and shaded her fingernails.

Lyndee Rae apologized. "Kurt has a Zoom meeting today. Are you sure this is okay?"

Di closed the door behind them. "Of course. I said you could bring her."

"Honey, this is Miss Di. Can you say thank you for letting you come today?"

Paisley muttered her thanks, clearly more interested in surveying the room.

Di squatted to the girl's level. "I'm glad you could visit, sweetie. What did you bring with you today?"

The girl unzipped the pack and emptied it onto the floor. A story book, a coloring book with a box of crayons, and two dolls fell out, one fully clothed, the other completely naked. "This is Sadie." She held up the undressed doll, then the other one. "And this is Clarissa."

"I see. Are they sisters? Or friends?"

Paisley put a finger to her mouth and thought a moment.

"Cousins." She knelt on the floor and proceeded to remove Clarissa's clothes.

"Won't she be cold without her clothes on?"

"No, she's hot."

Di grinned up at Lyndee Rae, who rolled her eyes.

"She does this with all her dolls."

Di stood and murmured, "I'm sure male dolls would find those ladies pretty hot."

They snickered, then Di turned to the day's priorities.

"I still have some boxes to go through in Eva's room. Do you want to start on one of the other bedrooms?"

Lyndee Rae agreed and checked to see if Paisley wanted to stay and play in the living room or come back with her.

"Can I play the piano?" The girl stood at the piano with a nude Clarissa poised over the keyboard.

"If Miss Di says it's okay."

"As long as you play it gently," Di said, "and don't pound on the keys."

Paisley lowered her doll and walked her across the ivories from one end. "Like this?" High musical notes sounded, reminiscent of a bird hopping along a window.

"That's perfect. Thank you for asking."

The women turned toward the bedrooms accompanied by deepening notes that thudded ever lower.

Lyndee Rae stopped at the first doorway. "Have you found anyone to take the piano?"

"No one. I've called schools, churches, and a couple of people who give lessons to see if they knew of anyone wanting a free piano. I even offered it to a store that sells pianos, but they wouldn't take it either."

"Maybe put an ad in the paper or on social media?"

"One of the piano teachers told me people don't want pianos anymore because music is so readily available. Besides that, they're expensive instruments, heavy, and take up a fair amount of space. Keyboards are more popular because they occupy less space and can be stored away. They also cost less and offer a variety of sounds."

Lyndee Rae frowned. "Sad. I hated piano lessons when I was young, but it's so basic to all other instruments." She watched Paisley, still walking her doll across the keys. "I'd love to take it, but we don't have room for it."

"You're not missing any great opportunity. It's so out of tune, I'm embarrassed to even give it away. Not sure it's really usable." And what then? What if she couldn't fulfill Eva's last wish? Nothing terrible would happen if she failed to find someone to treasure Eva's old piano. Except she'd feel terrible for having failed her mother. Again.

With a shrug, Lyndee Rae turned to the bedroom. "I'm sure you'll find someone who wants it. Now what else are we looking for?"

———

Di carried the box she'd set aside out to her car's trunk, then called a break time. She removed a small carton of milk from the fridge and opened the box of doughnuts on the table. Paisley climbed onto a chair and leaned forward on her knees to choose a doughnut.

Di pushed them closer to her. "Do you like frosted ones or glazed?"

Paisley licked her lips. "I like all of them."

"Just one, Paisley." Lyndee Rae came from the bedroom holding the remnant of a potted plant. "I know you weren't going to bother with throwing things out, but I think this deserves a proper burial." The crinkled stem of what was once a philodendron flopped to one side like a deflated tube dancer from Mitch's dealership. Its dried brown leaves disintegrated when touched. Lyndee Rae held one hand underneath to catch the crumbles.

"Take it out to the back yard." Di opened the door to let her out.

Mouth rimmed in chocolate frosting, Paisley looked toward the ceiling. "What's that noise?"

Before Di could answer, Lyndee Rae poked her head inside. "Want to see a helicopter, honey? Come look."

Paisley scrambled down from the table, licking her sticky fingers, and ran outside where Lyndee Rae picked her up and pointed. The chopper hovered above the trees a few blocks away, the sunlight glinting off its blades.

Di joined them, watching as it lifted and slowly rotated in a full circle, then turned and flew away.

"What is it doing, Mommy?" Paisley's head rested on Lyndee Rae's shoulder.

"Probably the men who are going to build new houses here." She brushed her hand across the girl's face and headed inside. "Are you getting tired?"

Di listened until the beating of the rotors faded away. Was Scott in that copter? Did she only imagine it hesitated briefly while facing this direction? Might he still harbor some affection for her? The idea sent her pulse thumping in time with the disappearing chopper's propellers. How would she react if he—?

"Di, it's Paisley." Lyndee Rae's frantic cry spilled through the doorway. "... the hospital."

10

"Shouldn't we call an ambulance?" Di unlocked the car and moved the box on the back seat to the floor.

"We've been through this before. I don't want to wait." Lyndee Rae laid an unconscious Paisley on the seat and stuffed a pillow under her legs, raising them above her head. "Sometimes her heart doesn't pump enough blood to the brain. I'll monitor her pulse while you drive."

Di broke nearly every traffic law getting to the hospital while Lyndee Rae alerted the ER and kept them apprised of Paisley's vital signs. The medical team took over as soon as they drove up to the door. Lyndee Rae followed them.

Di parked the car, then looked for her in the waiting room. But of course, she was with Paisley, and the receptionist asked her to wait.

Was it only two weeks since their roles had been reversed with Lyndee Rae offering her moral support? No wonder she knew what to do with Eva. And here Di sat unable to provide the least bit of comfort and assurance. But what did she know anyway about little girls' needing heart transplants? She was no help at all.

A man rushed in from outside and asked for Paisley or Lyndee Rae. He glanced at Di as she approached.

"Kurt? You're Lyndee Rae's husband? I'm Di Lange. I brought her and Paisley here."

"Oh, yes, thank you." Breathless, he swiveled his head back and forth between Di and the receptionist as if unsure who to pay attention to. The door to the exam rooms opened and a nurse called his name. He excused himself, but Di caught his arm.

"I won't stay now that you're here. Just let Lyndee Rae know—"

"Yes, yes, I will." He pulled away and raced through the door that closed behind him and locked with a *scrtch*.

Di returned to Eva's house. She still had all afternoon to sort through boxes, but fatigue soon replaced the adrenaline rush. Sinking onto a chair at the table, she stared at what was left of Paisley's doughnut. She'd never had to face the prospect of losing a child. Her own loss was still fresh but how could an elderly parent's death compare to that of a little one?

It had been a long time since she'd prayed. Intentionally, at least. Or had she ever been serious about praying? Maybe that's why she never saw any results, why she let the habit slip. Would God listen now? She wasn't asking anything for herself, but for that precious young life and for her parents. Di closed her eyes, but no words came. Only a torrent of tears.

She grabbed napkins to soak up the grief, then closed the box of untouched doughnuts and put them in the refrigerator. Maybe they'd keep until Sunday when the kids would be here. Paisley's doughnut and milk carton went into the trash. With great effort, she forced herself to sort through more boxes in Eva's bedroom.

The sun was low enough to shine directly through the bedroom window when her phone signaled a call from Lyndee Rae.

"How's Paisley?" Di was almost afraid to ask.

"Better. She's awake and asking for her doughnut."

Di exhaled her relief and laughed. "I just threw it in the trash."

"We won't tell her." Lyndee Rae chuckled. "Hey, thanks for breaking the speed limits to get us here. I'm sorry I won't be back today. I need to stay with Paisley. Probably tomorrow, too."

"I wouldn't hear of you coming back so soon."

"We'll need to pick up my car but we can do that on our way home."

"I might see you. I'm planning to work here a little longer since I have an appointment tomorrow morning. I'll be back here in the afternoon, and my family offered to help on Sunday, so don't feel like you need to rush back. Take care of that sweet little girl and tell her I'll buy a special doughnut just for her the next time she comes."

"Thank you, Di. You have no idea how much this means to us."

Di cut the call and peered at the rest of the boxes. There weren't that many, but she'd had enough. She went out to the kitchen and took stock of the pantry and the cupboards. Would a doll, a vase, or a painting be found among food stuffs or kitchen appliances? Doubtful. Still, what a shame to leave all this for destruction. Maybe she should have an estate sale. Could she organize and pull one off in less than three weeks? Of course she could—she was a professional organizer. Forego pricing and simply let customers make an offer. What a tempting idea!

Before leaving, she searched the two bathrooms and

removed all the prescription and over-the-counter medicines. She'd drop them off at a pharmacy for disposal. Eva's lotions, shampoos, powders, and makeup all went into the trash with the half-eaten doughnut. She breathed a simple prayer for Paisley's recovery.

"Thank you."

Sitting on the living room floor that evening, Di passed a black-and-white photo to Julianna. "Here's one of Grand Eva and Grandpa Walt."

"Is that Aunt Glori too?"

Di looked again. "It sure is. Good catch."

"I wish I could've known Grandpa Walt."

"He was thrilled when you were born. Showed you off to everyone he could." Di shuffled through several more photos from the box she'd brought home and pulled one out. "Look. Here's Grandpa Walt holding you just a few days after you were born."

Julianna studied it, holding it as if she could reach through time and touch her grandfather. "Can I keep this?"

"Sure."

She held it to her heart, then set it atop an end table before rummaging through the box. Julianna held up a yellow rope with tassels on the ends. "An honor cord. Grand Eva's or Grandpa Walt's?"

Di shrugged. "I'd guess Eva's. Dad wasn't much for keeping things like that."

Julianna extracted a school picture from the box and laughed. "That's Grand Eva? Look at those glasses."

"Cat-eye glasses. Very popular when she was about your age—maybe a little older—right along with bobby sox and poodle skirts. By the time she was in college, kids were into bell-bottom jeans and tie-dye shirts. And by then, most people who could afford it exchanged their glasses for contact lenses." Di reached into the box and brought out a silver wrist bracelet. "Hey, look at this."

"What is it?"

"A POW bracelet."

"What is that? Whose name is that?"

"During the Vietnam war, whenever one of our soldiers was taken prisoner by the North Vietnamese army, his name was inscribed on a bracelet like this. People here at home bought them and wore them until the soldier was released and came home. Or was declared dead."

Julianna examined the bracelet, reading the inscription out loud. "Humbert Roque Versace. Did he ever come home?"

"I don't know. We'll have to look up his name."

Julianna fitted the bracelet around her wrist then dug through the box again and came up with a class ring. "Is this Grand Eva's ring from the university?"

"It looks too big. Maybe Grandpa Walt's?"

"There's some initials engraved on the inside." Julianna turned the ring sideways to catch the best light and peered at the writing. "EC." She scrunched her eyebrows together. "Shouldn't it be EM for Eva Malone?"

"Her maiden name was Chapman."

"Oh-h." Julianna nodded and after trying the ring on various fingers, she settled it on her thumb. "You're right. It must've been Grandpa Walt's. This would never fit Grand Eva's fingers. But how romantic that he engraved her initials inside his ring." She blew on it and rubbed it against her shirt. "The gold still shines." Her head tipped to one side, a puzzled expression spreading across her face. "Why do you think it was in here and not in her jewelry box?"

"Good question. Maybe it didn't mean as much to her once they got engaged." Di tossed a few programs and other odds and ends back into the box and folded the flaps over it. "The rest of this stuff seems to be from her high school and college days. We'll hang on to the photos and maybe one of the yearbooks. Anything else you want to keep?"

"Nope." Julianna held up her wrist with the bracelet and her thumb with the ring. "It might be fun to track this guy down and send him the bracelet, if he's still alive. And I think the ring should go in Grand Eva's jewelry box."

Di considered canceling Friday morning's client appointment, but it was one of two that had been on the schedule since before Eva's death. She'd pushed all others beyond the demolition date so she could give the house her full attention.

Lauren Todd welcomed Di into her condominium and led her to the bathroom with its cluttered vanity.

"I'm usually more orderly than this." Lauren grimaced at the overflow of perfume bottles, mascara tubes, lip gloss, a blow dryer, and more. "I swear, I have no trouble keeping my business organized. So, why can't I keep a neat bathroom?"

Di sized up the situation. "Let's get this cleaned up and organized. Then I'll give you some tips to keep it that way. What kind of business are you in?"

"Wedding planning." Lauren followed Di's instructions, separating like items and throwing away any that were out of date or used up.

Di gathered bottles of foundation and a few eyeliner pencils. "Have you always loved weddings?"

Lauren laughed. "I used to enjoy them more than I do now.

Since I'm not married, I never imagined what all went into planning weddings these days."

"Do you have your own venue?"

"I just bought an old fixer-upper, mainly because of the big backyard. My dad's going to help renovate the house, and with some quick work, I think we'll have the outside ready in a month or so for small weddings. Eventually, I hope to offer indoor ceremonies with outdoor receptions or vice versa." She slid some used compacts into the trash bag. "For now, I work as a liaison between the bride and other venues."

"Do you have a piano for your venue?" Di checked a tube of lipstick, then put it in the throw-away bag. "If not, I can offer you one at a price you can't beat."

Lauren wrinkled her nose. "Sorry. We'll use canned music unless the bride prefers live. In that case, she'll choose the ensemble."

Di set several plastic organizer trays on the bed and transferred the reduced collections of cosmetics into them. "How many bridezillas have you encountered?"

Lauren rolled her eyes. "Too many. Their mothers are even worse. If anything could make me want to quit, that would be it. When the two of them disagree and I'm stuck in the middle, it's a nightmare. Do I satisfy the bride or the mother who's got the money?"

After they finished, Lauren admired all her hygiene and beauty products neatly in place. "I don't want to use it and mess it up."

"Remember, I offer refreshers three-to-six months later. You know where to find me."

"No offense, but I hope I won't have to take you up on that."

Di headed for the door. "Are you sure I can't interest you in a piano?"

Lauren tipped her head. "Maybe. Let me think about it."

"Don't wait too long." As in two weeks or less. What if she couldn't find a taker before Scott destroyed the house? An estate sale was sounding more and more like a possible answer.

Distant thunder growled as Di walked out to her car. She stopped at home for lunch, grabbed more trash bags and drove to Eva's house. The occasional thunder still hadn't brought any needed rain. In Eva's front yard, the patchy grass exposed several half-inch wide cracks in the parched ground. But the clouds looked lower and heavier so maybe the dry spell would be over soon. She parked in the driveway under the live oak tree and dragged the emptied garbage bins up from the street to the side of the house. The trash collectors had more than earned their pay this week.

The sight of Eva's empty chair as she entered always brought a hollow ache to her chest. She ignored the tightening in her throat. At least the living room no longer held all that clutter, not that it would matter once the house was demolished. But Sunday, Julianna and Namiko could use this area to sort through whatever they brought down from the attic.

A quick search of the kitchen cupboards and pantry turned up some small appliances that could go in the estate sale—Eva's toaster, electric mixer, a slow cooker, and a blender. The pots and pans showed their age, and the cake and cookie pans had grown rusty. On Sunday, she'd put Aunt Glori in charge of the kitchen and let her figure out what people might want to buy. Today, she intended to finish off Eva's bedroom.

At the closet, she stepped onto a stool to better see what was on the top shelf—purses, hats, silk scarves. She examined one scarf with a colorful geometric pattern that she remembered Eva wearing. They all looked to be in good shape, but did anyone wear these anymore? She folded and set them aside, stuffing most of the rest into the trash bag, including the worn shoes and sandals that littered the floor.

With the closet cleaned out, Di closed the door, then got down on her knees to check under the bed. She let out a moan. Of course—four plastic storage bins. At least they were covered, but as she pulled one out, she had to brush away a decade's worth of cobwebs. The air churned with dust, and a sneezing fit sent her on a search for tissues. She found the box in a bathroom cupboard and brought it out to the kitchen. Now if she could find the vacuum, she'd use it on those bins before going any further.

She blew the dust from her nose then reached to drop the tissue in the wastebasket. At the last minute, she jerked her hand away from the trail of ants crawling into and out of the container. Di lifted the lid and found Paisley's frosted doughnut swarming with ants.

"Augh!" She dropped the tissue on top of them, then carried the basket outside. Avoiding as many of the annoying little pests as possible, she tied the ends of the plastic liner bag together, lifted it and dropped it into one of the trash bins. She turned the kitchen can upside down and knocked it against the ground to get rid of any remaining ants. There should be some spray in the garage to take care of any pests left inside.

A white pickup rolled past on the street, stopped, then backed up and parked. It sported a heavy brush guard in front and a King Ranch medallion on the side. The driver got out and strode toward her.

"Scott?"

11

The sight of him quickened her pulse. Her heart danced a little two-step while her stomach tightened. What was he doing here? Had he come looking for her? What would Mitch think?

"Hey, Diamond. Was driving through and saw you outside. Figured I'd stop a minute." He inched his hat upward with his thumb and took in the house and yard with a smile. "Sure brings back memories."

She followed his gaze, trying to size up the neighborhood as one would after being away so many years. "It's definitely seen better days, hasn't it? I guess tearing it down and starting over isn't such a bad idea after all."

He turned sympathetic eyes toward her. "You've got a lot more memories tied up here than I do. I'm sorry if I've seemed callous."

Di brushed away his apology. "I'd been trying for years to get Eva to move. I guess it's hard to lose my old stomping grounds now that I've lost her too." She shifted the waste basket from one hand to the other. "What do you remember most?"

Lightning flashed and they both ducked at a thunderous explosion. Fat raindrops cascaded from the sky. Hand on her back, Scott urged her toward the door, and they ran for cover.

Inside, water poured onto the floor mat as he removed his hat. His mouth formed a smirk, but his eyes twinkled. "I don't remember the neighborhood being quite so shocking. Or damp."

Di grinned. "Let me get some towels." She set the waste basket to the side, shook the rain from her arms, and hurried to the bathroom where she searched for a couple bath towels that were less worn than the others. Mitch's warning to be careful rang in her ears as she handed one to Scott.

He rubbed the moisture from his hat and shoulders and perused the room. "Looks pretty much the same as I remember it."

Di considered whether to offer him the couch or a chair at the table. Dangerous thoughts wriggled into her imagination with the couch, so she invited him to the dining area. "Would you like anything to drink? We have water or water."

He grinned and took a seat. "Don't bother. I'm fine."

"So, tell me what comes to mind." Would any of his special memories include her? She sat across from him.

He drummed his fingers. "Well, let's see. I remember your dad coming out to threaten me the first time I picked you up for a date."

Di protested. "He did not threaten you. Dad never threatened anyone."

He chuckled and scratched his head. "I know that now but that's what it felt like. He was pretty protective of you, but that's not a bad thing. What else? The Friday night get-togethers after the games and Eva welcoming us with cookies and goodies. She was amazing."

"She loved having crowds of kids here." Di studied his expressions as he reminisced and found traces of the teenage Scott behind his facial hair.

"I remember our cars lining the street so no one could get through, and all of us chasing each other through the neighbors' yards for a game of tag or something. Hard to believe no one called the police with all the yelling and screaming we did."

"Ever thought about moving back?"

Scott shook his head. "There were some good times, but I couldn't wait to get out of here."

"Why?"

He looked at the rain pelting the window. "I needed to get away from home." He glanced at her then dropped his gaze to the table. "My mother was an alcoholic."

She caught her breath and blinked. "She was? How did I not know that?"

"You weren't supposed to know. We didn't talk about stuff like that back then." He dipped his chin and chewed the tips of his mustache that hung onto his lip. "She got mean when she drank. Dad wasn't easy to get along with either. I don't know if it was his disappointment with Mom or the pressure of keeping her secret." He shrugged and looked up again. "Anyway, I left, got my degree, tried the military for a few years, and now I'm running my own show." He leaned his elbows on the table. "What about you? You're married. Kids?"

Be careful.

"One. A daughter. You?"

"Nah, I tried it once. Marriage, I mean. Nice woman, but she wanted me home. I'm just not cut out for that life. My work takes me away from home a lot. I'd rather be out on the job with my crew than sitting home watching TV every evening."

Di frowned. "Doesn't that get lonely when they go home to their families?"

He played with the brim of his hat on the table. "I have a lady friend back in Austin. She's a flight attendant. International. We understand each other, get together when we're both in town and available." He shrugged one shoulder. "It works."

She thought she knew him so well way back when. In truth, she'd known him far less than she should have for someone she'd planned to marry someday. And what kind of life would she have had if those dreams had come true? Disappointment, loneliness, divorce . . . Maybe if his home life had been better while growing up, but that too was a revelation for her. Her attraction to him dissolved in a pool of reality.

He patted his pocket, then stood and reached for his hat. "Must've left my phone in the truck. I should get going. They're probably wondering what happened to me, not that they can do much in this rain. By the way, did you see my helicopter checking out the neighborhood the other day?"

"We did." Di came around the table to see him out. "You don't use a drone?"

"I like seeing things for myself. Learned to fly in the service, transporting injured soldiers from the battlefield in Iraq. Once my company got profitable, I got myself a chopper." He dropped his hat onto his head.

"*You* were flying it?"

"Yes, ma'am." He laid his arm on her shoulders and gave her a side hug. "Anytime you want a ride, you let me know."

The door burst open, and Julianna stumbled in, dripping wet. "Mom, whose truck—" Her eyes grew wide as her gaze traveled from her mom to Scott's arm to Scott.

Di ducked away and handed her a towel. Her heart pounded at the thought of the wrong story getting back to Mitch. "Julianna, this is my friend, Scott Jones. Scott, my bedraggled daughter, Julianna."

Scott laughed and held out his hand to shake. "Pleased to meet you, Julianna. You're just as pretty as your mama, even soaking wet."

Julianna blushed as she gave a brief shake, then scrubbed the towel over her hair.

Scott touched two fingers to the brim of his hat. "Nice talking with you, Diamond. Until next time. And Julianna, I hope to see you again too. Y'all take care." He pulled the door closed behind him, leaving an awkward silence in the room.

Julianna's voice wavered underneath the towel. "Did I interrupt something?"

"No, dear. Your timing was perfect. There's nothing you need to worry about."

She let the towel slip to her shoulders. "Really?"

Di met her narrowed eyes with confidence. "Really."

Julianna moved to the window and watched the truck drive away. "He must've been awfully hot when you dated. Is he married now?"

"No. Well, yes. He's married to his work."

Julianna turned from the window and hurried to the bathroom, throwing a suspicious glance at Di on the way.

Di's fingers went to her necklace. She ran her tongue over her lower lip. What would it take to convince her daughter she wasn't cheating on her marriage? Before the story got to Mitch.

The butterflies Scott stirred in Di's stomach must have reproduced caterpillars. They gnawed away at her insides during that evening's supper with an unusually quiet Julianna.

Mitch passed the basket of garlic bread and asked, "How was school today, Cinderella?"

"Okay." Julianna shrugged and trailed her fork around her plate of spaghetti.

"How's the play coming along?"

"Fine." Her answer carried all the enthusiasm of a Monday morning exam.

"You and Namiko have any special plans this evening?"

Another shoulder hitch. "Maybe."

Mitch studied her a moment, then tried another tack. "Did Mom tell you she talked with the university's Art Department chair, and she's interested in your idea for Eva's memorial?"

Her eyes flicked toward Di, then back to her plate, staring at it as if the noodles might wiggle off onto the floor.

"O-kay." Mitch cleared his throat and quirked an eyebrow at Di.

She faked a sympathetic smile and concentrated on her own food. She needed to come clean with him about Scott's visit, even though there wasn't much to tell. It was completely innocent.

Sure, he'd given her a side hug. But the way Julianna was acting, you'd think she caught them locked in a passionate embrace. Scott hadn't made any suggestive comments or acted in any way inappropriately. They were just two old friends reminiscing about days long gone.

True, he was still an attractive man, and she enjoyed his attention. If she were single, he'd be a major temptation. But that secret corner of her heart he'd occupied all these years was shrinking fast. All the little fantasies she'd constructed in her mind over the years evaporated like mist in sunlight. He wasn't worth jeopardizing her marriage over. Or her relationship with Julianna. Mitch needed to hear the facts from her before he learned about Scott's visit from their suspicious but misguided daughter.

Forty minutes later, Di put the last of the dinner plates and silverware into the dishwasher. Namiko stood in the doorway.

"Did Julianna tell you we're going to a birthday party at Lindsay's house?"

Di straightened and pushed the start button. "No, she didn't. Thank you for letting me know."

"I'll be sure to have her home before midnight."

"We appreciate that, Namiko. You know you can call us if anything comes up."

"Yes, thank you. Have a good evening." He smiled and followed Julianna—who gave Mitch a terse goodnight and completely ignored Di—out the door. Maybe the young man's polite manners would rub off on her daughter.

Mitch took Namiko's place in the kitchen doorway. "What's with her? Is it that time of the month?"

If only it were that simple.

"She got the wrong idea about something she saw."

Mitch frowned. "And she's taking it out on you? What happened?"

Di pressed her hand to her stomach as the caterpillars took a big chomp.

"I'm finished here. Let's go sit on the couch where it's more comfortable." She led him into the living room and perched beside him, angling her body to face him. She took his strong, warm hand between both of hers.

"You need to know that Scott showed up at Eva's house while I was cleaning today."

His eyes narrowed. "What do you mean, he showed up?"

"Just what I said. I was outside, he drove by and saw me and stopped to chat. I wasn't going to invite him in, but a sudden deluge sent us running for cover. We stayed at the dining room table and reminisced about the neighborhood, what life was like there when we were growing up." Di stared at the rug without focusing on it. "He said his mother was an alcoholic. I can't believe I never knew."

"We miss a lot of adult stuff when we're young," Mitch said. "Where does Julianna figure into this?"

"After about twenty minutes, Scott got up to leave and gave me a side hug. That's when Julianna stumbled in out of the rain and saw his arm around my shoulders. It seems she didn't believe me when I told her there was nothing going on between us."

"A side hug, huh? That's pretty serious." A half-smile at his mouth told her he was being sarcastic. "You having an affair with this guy?"

"Would I be telling you this if I was?"

Mitch tipped his head in a thoughtful pose. "Maybe, if you wanted to head off anything Julianna might tell me."

"Neither of us said or did anything inappropriate. I hope you know me better than that by now."

"I do," he said, squeezing her hand. "But let me ask you something, just for my own curiosity. Are you attracted to him?"

Di inhaled a long breath through her nose. "I admit I was. At first. But I think I'm attracted to what was, back when we were teenagers, to that eighteen-year-old boy I used to know."

She snorted. "We're grown now. He's changed. I've changed. I don't know this bearded man with his own construction company. I thought I knew him so well when we were dating, but . . . I realize now that I knew nothing. I was only sixteen, Julianna's age. As serious as my feelings were for him, we were practically strangers."

She brought Mitch's hand to her lips and kissed it. "I love

you, Mitch. You're the one I vowed to remain faithful to, and I fully intend to keep that vow."

He cupped her cheek. "I love you, too, Diamond. You're worth everything to me and more."

His words expelled every caterpillar in her stomach. He leaned forward and kissed her.

"What about Julianna?" Di asked when they separated. "She obviously didn't believe me when I told her there was nothing to worry about. Maybe you could talk to her?"

"Sure." Mitch let go and stretched back with his hands behind his head. "I'll tell her I don't mind you having a boyfriend as long as he shares half the bills and pays for her college."

12

A bulldozer, a front-end loader, and an excavator took up half a block where houses once stood.

They tore at Di's heart as Mitch drove past on the way to Eva's on Sunday. The pastor's sermon this morning was all about building houses on rock versus sand. What happens when what seemed like rock turns to sand, and your once-beloved home is lost forever?

Just over a week ago, Scott's estimate allowed her two to three weeks. At best she had a couple weeks left. At worst, only seven days in which to find a painting, a vase, and a doll.

Mitch parked in Eva's driveway and followed Di to the door carrying a box of doughnuts.

"If you don't find the rest of the stuff on Eva's list, then what?" he asked.

Di juggled more trash bags and gloves to unlock the front door. "I will have failed my mother."

"She'll never know."

"But I will. She already questioned my choice of professions. If I can't even carry out her last wish, maybe I should take up basket weaving instead." She stepped inside and held the door for Mitch.

"You're too hard on yourself, sweetheart. If they tear the house down, I'd say you have a legitimate reason for giving up the quest." He set the box of pastries on the table and in the voice of a television announcer said, "You could be the next winner of a dozen fresh doughnuts in the Sunday afternoon clearing house sweepstakes."

Grinning, Di brought out the ones left from Friday. "Try one of these and tell me if they're still good."

Mitch selected one of the glazed ones and took a couple bites. "A little dry, but not bad. Warm them up a bit and no one will know."

"Good idea. I'll wait until they get here. With everyone coming to help today, I figured the least I can do is give them a sugar high." She went through the rooms turning on lights and setting out gloves and wastebaskets in the work areas.

Mitch swallowed the last bite of his doughnut.

"Think Scott'll show up again?"

"It's possible." How would Mitch react if he did? Her confession about holding onto the memory of Scott's affections for so long had been freeing. She'd wronged Mitch by withholding that small part of her heart, but no more. Finally, she could honestly regard Scott as merely an old friend. She swept a lone hair from her face and turned to him. "How should we handle it if he does?"

Mitch rinsed the crumbs from his hands at the kitchen sink and gave his mouth a swipe.

"Send him to me," he said, before heading out to the garage.

The door barely closed behind him when Aunt Glori opened the front door. Julianna and Namiko followed her inside.

"All that heavy equipment," Gloria said. "It's really happening, isn't it? I guess I shouldn't be sad. The new houses will be much more profitable real estate."

"But Grand Eva's house," Julianna wailed. "I'll never be able to come here again." The box on the table provided a welcome distraction. "Ooh, doughnuts!" She raced to grab a strawberry-frosted goodie and offered a chocolate one to Namiko. He turned it down.

Aunt Glori refused, too. "I've gained a couple pounds just looking at them. Diamond, where do you want me?"

"Start with the bathrooms, then the kitchen. I've decided to hold a name-your-price estate sale, so whatever you think someone might want, set it aside. I'm more interested in getting rid of usable items than making money. Everything else goes in the trash. And remember, we're still looking for a teal floor vase, a star painting, and a rag doll."

Aunt Glori nodded and disappeared into the nearest bathroom.

"Namiko and I have the attic. Right, Mom?" Julianna licked the frosting from her fingers. Her attitude had vastly improved after Mitch talked with her.

"Yes, and thank you both for helping. Especially you, Namiko. It's very kind of you."

"You're most welcome." He bobbed his head. "Glad to help."

Di went to the hall and pulled on the rope to lower the attic stairs. "Here you go. Move everything down to the living room first. It'll be easier to sort in this light. But watch for mice and other critters."

Julianna cringed and pushed Namiko's shoulder. "You go first."

He grinned, then scrambled up the stairs.

With everyone occupied, Di squeezed around the attic

stairway and busied herself with the hall closet where she'd found the vacuum cleaner on Friday. After moving it out of the way, she withdrew coats, an umbrella, a suitcase fully loaded with rolls of paper towels and toilet paper, and a walking cane. Had Eva ever used a cane? It looked brand new. Di would bet money a doctor had ordered it for her, and she'd refused to use it. She shook her head and continued digging through the closet's contents. One storage box held letters, postcards, and other memorabilia. Another box farther back held a flashlight and batteries. What was the point of storing it in such an out-of-the-way place?

From the guest bathroom, Aunt Glori called, "Hey! Look what I found. I can't believe Eva kept these."

Julianna descended the stairs, set a crate on the floor, and peeked at the contents of the slim white box Gloria held out. "Are those teeth?"

Coming out from behind the stairway, Di took the box and looked closely. "My baby teeth, molars and all."

"Eww." Julianna backed away, her hand covering her mouth.

Di replaced the cover and handed the box back to Gloria. "I think we can safely assume no one will pay for those."

Aunt Glori dropped the box in the trash, and Di returned to the closet with a long-forgotten memory of her first loose tooth coming to mind. Every day, Dad asked to wiggle it until one night, the tooth fell into his hand without a trace of the accompanying pain she'd imagined. The next morning, a shiny new quarter lay under her pillow, her tooth gone, never to be seen again. Until today.

Wasn't that just like Eva? Holding onto baby teeth while caring little for things of real value like the expensive artwork decorating her walls. Di ground her teeth as she dug more junk out of the hall closet. The hours she and others had spent searching for Eva's worthless treasures should instead be spent disposing of items that mattered. Who would want an old ceramic vase or doll? Even the piano held little value. Who would treasure it the way Eva wanted? And what in the world was the star painting? A nativity scene?

The door to the garage opened with a squeak, and Mitch called to her. "Hey, Di? Can you come out here for a minute?"

She set a shoebox full of photos on the floor and went out to the garage. Mitch had raised the overhead door to let in light and air.

"I want to show you something." He led her past lawn equipment and bicycles. A hula hoop and roller skates rested atop her dad's old workbench. Mitch pointed to a dusty ceramic floor vase holding peacock feathers in various stages of disintegration. A hand-molded leaf pattern adorned the shoulders between side handles. "Could this be the one on your list?"

Di's fingers explored the leaf pattern on the shoulders. With her thumb, she scraped a thick layer of dust from one of the side handles.

"It's a floor vase. And that looks like teal to me. Congratulations! You've just won the box of doughnuts." She threw her hands in the air, then pulled him close and kissed his cheek.

His arm wound around her back to pull her close. His smile warmed her. A good sign that maybe this whole thing with Scott had blown over.

"Three items down," she said. "Only two more to go."

Mitch scanned the garage. "I should move it outside, so I don't knock it over while I'm clearing out all the other stuff."

"It's probably brittle. If you'll clear a path, I'll carry it out."

He shoved a dented aluminum garbage can and a lawn mower aside, then insisted on lifting and moving the vase himself. Di supervised the relocation.

"Careful. Wait, let me get that rake out of your way." She held her breath until he set it down at the edge of the driveway. It didn't look like much, but she wasn't about to risk breaking it now that they'd finally found it. Get rid of those tattered peacock feathers and a good scrubbing should brighten it up like new.

Movement caught her eye, and she looked up to find Scott hurrying along the driveway.

"Need some help?" He strode up and offered his hand to Mitch. "Scott Jones. You must be Mr. Diamond?"

"Also known as Mitch." He side-eyed Di, smirked, and shook hands. "Looks like the demolition is underway."

"It is." Scott pushed his hat up and scratched his cheek whiskers. "Di might've told you I stopped by on Friday. After I left, I realized what a big job you're facing with a limited amount of time. Wondered if I can help in any way." He looked from Mitch to Di.

"I think we've got the inside covered." Di touched Mitch's arm. "What about out here, hon? Could you use a couple of extra hands?"

Mitch glanced toward the garage. "I won't turn 'em down."

Scott rubbed his palms together. "Tell me where to start, boss."

Di hurried inside, shut the door behind her and leaned against it. Would the two men play nice together? For a moment, she pictured an old-fashioned brawl, though Mitch's personality hardly fit that kind of scenario. Humorous digs would be more his style, the kind where the other guy isn't sure whether to take him seriously or not.

Aunt Glori interrupted her thoughts. "Everything okay out there?"

"Mitch found the vase."

"He did? I have to see it." She hustled toward the door.

"It's outside on the driveway. And he's got some help."

"Oh?"

"Scott Jones."

Gloria's eyes widened while her lips compressed in a straight line. "What's he doing here?" She assumed that familiar teacher look.

Di filled her in on Scott's previous visit and his stated reason for stopping by today.

"Mitch knows all about Scott and me. His sales experience makes him good at reading people. It's possible they'll hit it off, but if Mitch wants me to keep my distance, I will."

Aunt Glori nodded approval and went to look at the vase.

Namiko and Julianna descended the attic stairs, brushing dust and insulation from their clothes.

"I think we've got everything out, Mom. It was all Christmas stuff. Grand Eva had a ton of it."

"Thank you both for bringing it all down. If you want, you can look through everything and keep any ornaments you'd like. Check the lights, too, and throw out any that don't work."

"Can we set up her tree and decorate it?" Julianna bounced on her toes, her hands clasped in a pleading pose.

Di pursed her lips. "It might look like a Charlie Brown tree. I don't think she's used it in several years."

Namiko held up a shiny silver bell. "We'll cover it with ornaments to display for the sale."

Di nodded. "Okay. Go for it." The kids high-fived each other. "Before you start, go out and take a look at the vase Dad found in the garage."

"The teal one?" Julianna pumped her fist. "Yes! I want to see it."

"It's on the driveway."

Aunt Glori held the door open for their exit as she came

back inside. "I recognize that vase. Your mother made it for a class in college. It won a prize."

"What sort of prize?"

"Oh, I don't remember that. Too long ago, but she was awfully proud of it."

"She's done so much more since then. Wonder why she didn't choose one of her paintings or textile art?"

Aunt Glori shrugged. "As I recall, it was the first public recognition she received for her work."

Hands on hips, Di sighed. "Award-winning. That should help me find someone to treasure it, right?"

Back at the closet, she nearly had it cleared when Mitch called again from the garage.

"Di, we need you out here." His tone did not in any way match his previous call. He met her at the door.

"What's wrong?" She followed him outside. The kids had returned to their decorating, but Scott stood on the driveway, his head bowed.

"Diamond, I'm so sorry." Scott adjusted his hat so it covered more of his face. "We were moving lawn mowers and stuff around and . . . I backed into your vase."

It lay on its side on the concrete driveway, the base mostly intact, but the neck had broken loose and rolled off into the grass. A wide shoulder section was broken into three pieces with some of the leaves and one handle chipped off. A light breeze sent the peacock feathers hop-scotching down the pavement toward the street.

Di's shoulders sagged. If she thought before it would be hard to find someone who'd want it, this made it so much worse. Who would treasure a broken floor vase?

Mitch put his hands on his hips. "We can try to piece it back together. Get some strong ceramic glue."

Scott stared at the blue-green mash-up. "I should've looked where I was going."

Di bent to set the base upright and worked to keep her voice upbeat. "It's just a vase, not the end of the world. For now, put all the pieces inside the body here and move it farther out of the way. I'll decide what to do with it later."

Both men apologized again as they gently placed the shards into the base. Di held her tongue until she got back inside, then let out a growl. She might as well dump the vase. Maybe she'd suffer some horrible cosmic punishment for not fulfilling Eva's request, but who in the world would be interested in an old vase that's been pieced back together?

Aunt Glori tilted her head. "Now what?"

"I'm so tired of this. Everything will be demolished anyway, and Eva will never know if I kept a stupid promise or not." Di slapped her hand against the closed door.

Aunt Glori wrung out a rag and leaned against the counter, giving Di her full attention. "What's going on?"

"Am I a terrible daughter for breaking a promise I made to my dying mother? This treasure hunt we've been on is ridiculous. Nobody wants an out-of-tune piano or an old floor vase that's been broken and pieced back together."

"Whoa, whoa." Aunt Glori hung the rag on the faucet and jerked her head toward the garage. "What happened out there?"

"They bumped into the vase and broke it. Five or six pieces. Even if we can fix it, who's going to want it, much less treasure it?"

Julianna and Namiko came into the kitchen. While Julianna gathered a string of lights in her hands, Namiko's soft voice broke through the tension.

"Please. May I look at it?"

Di gestured, and the kids filed past her to the garage. The

men's voices drifted in through the open door. Arms crossed tight across her chest, Di stalked from room to room, gauging the progress they'd made. There was still so much to do, and the broken vase only complicated things. She never should've agreed to such a silly promise in the first place. She inhaled a deep, angry breath and exhaled her frustration, then made her way back to the kitchen where she met Namiko's shy gaze.

"Mrs. Lange, with your permission, I would like to have your vase."

"That's awfully sweet of you, Namiko, but you don't need to do that. We'll either try to glue it back together or just junk it."

"It's not as you imagine. I would very much like to have it."

Julianna chimed in. "Mom, it's perfect for a project in his art class at school. Please let him take it."

Why not?

"Okay. Go ahead. Better than leaving it here for the demolition crews. Ask your dad or Mr. Jones—"

"It's okay. We'll get it." Julianna tossed the light string into the living room and hurried out with Namiko at her heels.

Aunt Glori held up her hand with fingers spread. She folded her thumb and two fingers into her palm so that only two fingers remained up. "Three down, two to go."

Di rolled her eyes. "Giving it to a student for an art project hardly qualifies as giving it to someone who will treasure it."

"You never know."

———

Mitch opened the car door for Di, and she sank into the passenger seat. With all they'd accomplished today, she expected to feel satisfied. But so much more remained with only a week left. Before she knew it, the house where she grew up would be nothing more than a memory. She understood now the wistfulness in her grandparents' tales about their childhood homes.

Our house stood right in the center of that new medical center's parking lot.

That used to be the corner grocery store before they tore it down and built apartments.

Remember our old movie theater that sat where the bank is now? We'd all go to the Saturday matinees.

Someday, she'd tell her grandchildren a similar story. She leaned back against the headrest while Mitch started the car.

He squeezed her hand. "You look tired. Want to pick up something for supper?"

"Sure. Whatever you want."

He glanced at her. "You okay?"

"Generally speaking, yes."

"How about specifically?"

She exhaled a heavy breath. "Maybe I'm getting nostalgic, feeling the loss of my childhood home. Is progress always good? Isn't there some value in preserving the old neighborhoods with their history?" She peered out the window as they exited the neighborhood. "Nothing important happened here, except the daily lives of ordinary people. Isn't that worth something? Or is everything only meant for profit?"

Minutes passed before Mitch responded. "Maybe you should ask Scott those questions."

She gave him a side-eye, letting him know how little she thought of his suggestion.

He took her hand again, interlacing their fingers. "You have my permission to associate with him. I believe his intentions are honorable, but I would like to know about any time you see each other."

Di held up her right hand. "Guaranteed. Scout's honor."

Mitch smiled. "He's an interesting fella, done some impressive things with his life."

Di squeezed his hand and let go. "He is a nice guy. He was always friendly with everyone in school, and he treated me well." She'd dated other nice boys, too. Why had she held onto her affection for Scott all these years? What kept her from moving on from him the way she did when other relationships ended?

Mitch interrupted her thoughts. "He invited us both for a ride in his helicopter sometime. Are you interested?"

Leaning away, she turned to face him. "You do remember I'm afraid of heights, right?"

He shrugged. "You don't mind being in an airplane."

"I'm not crazy about airplanes either. But a helicopter has a huge picture window and a lot less to protect you if you crash. No thanks."

"Mind if I accept his invitation?"

"Not at all, as long as your life insurance is up to date before you climb aboard."

13

A phone call before 8:00 a.m. rarely meant good news, and never on Mondays. Di set her coffee cup on the kitchen table and reluctantly answered the call from one of her employees. "Courtney, what's up?"

"Me. All night in the bathroom."

"Ugh, I'm so sorry."

"I'd . . . try to find a sub . . . but I'm not sure . . . I can . . . stay out of the bathroom . . . that long."

"Anything I can do for you? Bring some soup—"

Courtney moaned.

"Oops, sorry. Remind me where you're scheduled today."

"Misty Ballard's." Another moan. "Gotta go." The call disconnected.

Poor thing. Di sipped her coffee and scrolled through her contact list. Most of her cleaning ladies were already scheduled for today. She called the others. One was out of town, and another had her grandbabies for the day. The rest had plans they couldn't or wouldn't cancel. She'd call Misty to reschedule as soon as she fortified herself with the coffee.

Some of her employees preferred a variety of different assignments, but others showed up week after week to the same households, often developing strong relationships with their regular customers. Courtney was one of those who loved knowing her clients, remembering important details, and giving them her best.

Misty answered the phone on the fourth ring.

"This is Di from Diamond Cleaning. I hate to be the bearer of bad news, but Courtney called in sick today—"

"Oh, no. What's wrong?" Genuine concern filled her voice.

"Sounded like either a stomach bug or food poisoning. Poor girl. She sounded really rough."

"I'm so sorry to hear that. Hope she feels better soon. Is someone else coming?"

"That's why I'm calling. Would you mind rescheduling for a different day? I haven't been able to find a sub."

"Oh no. Not this time. Isn't there anyone else you can send?"

"Ordinarily, yes, but I've gone through my whole list and can't find anyone to fill in."

Misty whined. "Ach, why today? I have out-of-town company coming this evening, and I was counting on Courtney. I don't have time to clean plus all the other prep work before they arrive. You're sure there's no one else?"

Di weighed her options. After working on Eva's house all yesterday afternoon, she'd promised herself a more leisurely morning. Over the years, she'd purposely separated herself from the cleaning part of the business. That didn't mean she couldn't do it. She simply preferred organizing. But to keep a client happy and not risk losing her ...

"Tell you what. Let me wrap up a couple of things here and I'll be there in about an hour. Will that work?"

"Yes, thank you. You're a life saver."

Di cut the call. With one week until Scott's crew bulldozed the house, she had little time to spend on other projects. Paperwork needed her attention too. She called Lyndee Rae.

"How's Paisley this morning?"

"As good as can be expected. Do you mind if I bring her to the house again?"

"Fine with me. I wondered if you'd be there today. I'm filling in for one of my employees this morning, but I gave you a key, didn't I?"

"Yes, I have it."

"I'm afraid my gang ate all the doughnuts yesterday."

Lyndee Rae laughed. "I'll be sure to bring our own snacks. Did y'all get a lot done?"

"You'll see. We didn't touch the bedroom you were working on so go ahead and start there. Call or text me if you need anything. I'll check in when I'm finished."

Di pulled on the required company t-shirt for cleaning, gathered her supplies, and soon approached the front door of a beautifully restored Neoclassical home on Colcord Avenue. Corinthian columns supported a second-floor balcony with extensive carved trim. Di whispered thanks she wouldn't have to clean that, but she wouldn't mind spending a summer evening sipping sweet tea on this welcoming wrap-around porch with its decorative railings and balustrades.

Misty opened the door before Di had a chance to ring the bell. "I can't thank you enough for this, Diamond. If you ever need a recommendation for a new client, send them to me. I'll make sure you get the business."

"That would be much appreciated." Di set her vacuum and bucket on the floor of the entry hall. A plush area rug protected the polished hardwood floors, and the chandelier above made the inside of the house every bit as elegant as the outside. She detected a faint vanilla scent, likely from a candle. "Any spots you especially want me to focus on today?"

Misty shook her head. "A good overall cleaning. My dad's living with me. He's in the downstairs bedroom. I'm going to run out and do some errands, if you don't mind. Dad shouldn't bother you at all unless you get him talking. Then he'll keep you here all day and into the night." She chuckled.

"What's his name?"

"Ed. Come and let me introduce you." Misty gestured for Di to follow. She knocked on a door that was ajar. "Are you decent, Dad?"

"As much as I'll ever be," answered a rusty voice from within.

Misty opened the door to what appeared to be a comfortable efficiency-style apartment, minus the kitchen. A white-haired gentleman turned his wheelchair from the television to face them. Misty went to sit on a chair beside him.

"Dad, Courtney's sick and can't make it today."

"Oh, I'm sorry to hear that." His shoulders drooped a bit, but the rest of his posture gave an impression of disciplined bearing.

"Di here is filling in for her. I wanted you to meet her before I leave."

He gave Di a once over. "Short for Diane?"

"No, sir. That's a reasonable guess, but it's short for Diamond." She bent toward him and shook his hand. "Nice to meet you, Mr. . . ."

"Cosley, but call me Ed." He gave a firm shake. "Diamond. What a unique name. Your parents must have considered you of great worth."

She gave him a bemused smile. "I'm sure there were times I was more like an expensive chunk of coal."

His eyes twinkled. "Be glad they didn't name you Pearl, an irritating grain of sand."

They all laughed.

Misty checked her watch. "I'm going out to get some extra groceries and supplies for tonight. Anything you need before I leave, Dad?"

"No, Diamond and I will get along just fine."

Misty got up and led Di out, stopping at his door. "You want this open or shut?"

"You can leave it open. When Di is ready to clean in here, she can come in without having to knock."

She walked Di back to the entryway. "I hope to be home by the time you finish the upstairs, but if I'm not, you can clean around Dad. He's used to Courtney being here. They talk and laugh like old friends." Misty picked up her purse and keys and exited out the back door.

Di didn't mind chatting with pleasant clients. It was the ones who complained about every little thing in their life that made her breathe a sigh of relief when she left. But they were usually the ones who most needed attention.

Today, she carried her cleaning supplies up the stairs and worked room by room dusting, straightening, and vacuuming. Ed's interpretation of her name made her chuckle and aroused the memory of a once popular song Dad claimed was written about her. After all these years, she could still hear his smooth tenor voice singing to her, calling her his Diamond girl.

She'd forgotten all but the first few lines, so she hummed it to herself while she cleaned, and made a mental note to look up the lyrics.

She'd give Courtney an A+ for her weekly cleaning. The ceiling fans, soap dishes, and baseboards all showed little accumulation, and Di finished the upstairs quicker than expected. Vacuuming the steps as she went down, she moved to the first floor. Misty apparently hadn't returned, but the television in Mr. Cosley's room was playing an old *Hogan's Heroes* episode. She started toward the kitchen when he called to her.

"Diamond. Come on in." He beckoned her with his fingers.

"I don't want to disturb your show."

"No need. I've seen it before. I'm sure I'll see it again."

She moved her mop and bucket into his bathroom. "I'll start in here so you can keep watching."

He flicked the television off and wheeled himself to the doorway. "I prefer human interaction, as long as you don't mind."

"Don't mind at all." Just like Eva. Why hadn't she spent less time taking care of business and more time visiting with her, filling that need for companionship and personal connection? She'd been so blind. It was too late to change her ways with Eva, but maybe she could make up for it in other ways.

"My daughter does her best to find ways for me to socialize outside the immediate family," he said, "but it's not like being able to get around on my own whenever the urge hits."

"How long have you lived here?" Di squirted cleaner into the toilet, then wiped down the walk-in shower.

Tipping his head back, he looked at the ceiling. "I guess it's about eight months. My back surgery failed, left me with partial paralysis. While I was in rehab, Misty and Rick moved upstairs and remodeled their master suite for me. They insisted I come live with them."

"I'm sure you'd rather be living independently, but you're lucky they were willing to do that. Have you always lived in the area?"

"No, I came from Oklahoma. Had an HVAC company there for about forty years before I retired. But I went to the university here in the late '60s, early '70s." He sat for a moment, shaking his head. "I have such good memories of my days there. Next fall will be our fiftieth reunion. I've only been to a handful of them when time and distance permitted, but it's always fun to reconnect with old college buddies." He rubbed the fingers on his right hand. "Wish I hadn't lost my ring."

Di moved on to scrub the sink and countertop. "Was that important when you were in school, getting your class ring?"

"Not so much as at other schools, like the Aggies. But I was a fifth-generation student here and my parents made sure I got one. Kids these days probably have better things to spend their money on, but for me it held special honor."

"How'd you lose it?"

"I didn't exactly lose it. I was pretty serious about a young lady when my draft number came up. I gave her my ring and told her to keep it until I returned." He rubbed his finger as if twisting a ring. "I spent some time on a Navy ship and by the time I came home, she'd married someone else. I didn't feel right asking her to give it back. With her new husband, I 'spect she simply forgot about it. Probably never gave it a second thought."

"That's too bad. You never ordered another one?"

"Nah. It wouldn't have meant as much."

She held up a scrub cloth in her gloved hand. "So, if you were drafted, that must've been the Vietnam war?"

"Yes, ma'am. Lot of boys didn't make it home again. Never have figured out why I was so lucky, but I thank the Lord for it every day."

Di loaded her car and glanced up at Misty's house before driving away. Chatting with the customers and their families was one of the perks of her business. Ed Cosley had made this job more interesting than most. She'd heard a little about the war from Dad and Eva—the nightly body count on the evening news, the protests, the peace movement. Eva never admitted it, but Di suspected she might have been one of those hippies they talked about, if even for a short time. A few relics showed up among the boxes in her bedroom. She couldn't imagine Dad ever wearing a tie-dye shirt with a peace symbol on it. And that beaded strap. Was it a headband or a choker?

Lyndee Rae's name came up on her Bluetooth screen and she answered the call. "Hey, I'm just leaving my morning job. Was going to pick up some lunch and then come to the house. How's it going?"

"Made some progress, but I'd like to take Paisley home and let her nap in her own bed."

"Will you be back later?"

"I hope so. I'll let you know either way. Oh, I think she found your doll."

"The Raggedy Ann?"

"Mm-hm. It was in the bottom of a laundry basket full of toys in that bedroom closet."

"Great. That means we only need to find the star painting."

"I'm afraid Ann's more raggedy than usual. One leg fell off and an arm is only hanging on by a few threads. A lot of her hair needs replacing too."

Di's enthusiasm dwindled. "Why am I not surprised? How will I pass off a doll like that?"

"I'm sure the leg can be reattached, and the arm only needs a couple stitches."

"Sewing has never been one of my many talents."

Lyndee Rae giggled. "Then let me take it home. I'll see what I can do."

"Have at it, girl. Thank you. And be sure you record your time for doing that."

14

Today is Tuesday.

Di went through a mental review of the week's coming events and noted them on her calendar.

Beginning tomorrow, Wednesday, Julianna's dress rehearsal.

Performance on Thursday.

Prep for the estate sale on Friday.

Sale on Saturday.

Time seemed to be slipping through her hands like a buttered potato squirting from her fingers. Only six days remained until the wrecking of Eva's house.

These past two weeks left her longing for the day when the house would no longer be her responsibility, her headache. Almost. Because when that day came, her familiar old neighborhood would be gone for good. And what if she couldn't find the painting by the time Scott's crew arrived?

She put those thoughts away as she parked outside a nondescript house in a starter-home neighborhood. Lyndee

Rae's car was in the shop and Di had offered to pick her up on the way. Rather than wait in the car, Di went to the door.

Kurt invited her inside. "She'll be right with you. She's saying goodbye to Paisley."

Unhappy voices rose from another room. "No, Mommy, she's mine."

"Honey, she's not yours. I brought her home to fix her, but we have to give her back."

"But I want her. Ple-ease." Paisley's voice grew more distraught.

"We'll find another one just like her."

"No! I love her. Don't—" The little girl screamed.

Kurt's cheeks flushed red. He dipped his head and excused himself, then hurried toward the commotion. A moment later, Lyndee Rae closed the door on the tantrum.

"Sorry you had to hear that." She handed the reconstructed Raggedy Ann to Di then picked up her purse and reached for the door handle. "I'm ready."

Di held the doll but looked at Lyndee Rae. "This is what she's upset about?"

Lyndee Rae's shoulders fell. "I didn't realize she'd think it was hers if we brought it home. I only meant to fix it."

Di pushed the doll back at Lyndee Rae. "Let her have it."

Holding her hands up in refusal, Lyndee Rae shook her head. "No. I don't want her to think—"

"Yes, let her keep it."

"Are you sure?"

"Absolutely. Eva wanted me to give these items to people who will treasure them. Paisley is the first and only one so far who fits that requirement."

Lyndee Rae pressed the doll back toward Di. "Then I want you to present it to her. Come on." She led the way to Paisley's room and knocked on the door. The girl's cries subsided into hiccups when Lyndee Rae peeked into the room and stepped aside to let Di enter.

Paisley sat on a pink Disney princess bedspread in the middle of a white four-poster bed. A high shelf held several prescription bottles. Next to the bed, a cardiac monitor and pulse and oxygen meter lay on the dresser above an oxygen tank.

Kurt released his hold on Paisley as Di knelt before her. The child's blue-tinged lips formed a downward curve, the lower lip extended in a pout. Tears clung to her lashes and streamed down her cheeks. She glanced at Di then fixed her gaze on Raggedy Ann.

"Paisley, I want to tell you a story. When my mother was a little girl like you, her sister gave her this doll. She loved her sister very much, but after a while, her sister got very, very sick and died."

Paisley sniffed. "Is she with Jesus?"

"Yes, I believe she is. But whenever my mother felt sad because she missed her sister, she turned to Ann here." Di held the doll up. "She loved Raggedy Ann so much that she kept her a secret from any of her friends and wouldn't share her with anyone. But when she grew very old and died, she wanted me to find someone to love Ann as much as she did."

Paisley swiped her eyes with the backs of her hands. Her chin trembled and her voice shook. "I love her."

"I know you do, sweetheart." Di put the doll into her arms. "She's yours to keep now. A special doll for a special little girl."

A tear crept down Paisley's cheek even as she smiled and hugged the doll close.

Kurt cleared his throat. "What do you say to Miss Di, Paisley?"

"Thank you." She rubbed her nose against the doll's half-bald head.

"You're welcome, sweetie. Take good care of her." Di rose and followed Lyndee Rae all the way out to the car. "I'm amazed she got so attached to that old thing in such a short time."

Lyndee Rae slid into the car's seat and waited until they were on their way. "Remember how she undresses all her dolls? When she found this one in that basket of toys, the first thing she did was take the clothes off."

Di chuckled, imagining the scene.

Lyndee Rae continued. "When she did, she noticed the embroidered heart on the doll's chest. Several of the threads are frayed and torn apart. She showed it to me and said—" her voice caught "—she said, 'She needs a new heart just like me.'"

Di's breath stalled. Tingles spread down her back. "Oh, my."

"I would've fixed the threads while I had it, but she wouldn't let me. She barely let go of it long enough for me to fix the arm and the leg. I thought I'd have to do it while she slept. But she especially wanted the heart to stay the same. 'Just like me,' she said."

Words failed her. Di braked in front of Eva's house. "Mother would be—" she searched for the exact description "—delighted, overjoyed, ecstatic." She smiled at Lyndee Rae. "All of the above."

Later that morning, a phone's jingle sounded. Di's cell wasn't in its usual spot. Where had she left it?

Lyndee Rae called from the other bedroom. "Want me to answer it?"

"Where'd I leave it?"

"Here." Lyndee Rae met her in the hall, holding the phone in the air like a trophy.

Di grabbed it and swiped the answer button. "Ah, too late."

"Anyone important?"

"Aunt Glori. I'll call her back later." She slipped the phone into her hip pocket only to have it jingle again. She checked the display. "This time it's a real estate agent I've done some work for." She swiped to answer it. "Hi, Jill."

"Hey, Di. Scott Jones, the guy whose apartment you set up, just called and asked me for your phone number. I didn't want to give it to him without your permission."

"Perfectly all right. Turns out we're old friends."

"No kidding?"

"Yep. Went to high school together. We've talked a couple of times since he got here. If it's any easier, you can text me his number and I'll get in touch with him."

Di waited for the text to come through, then sent Scott an emoji of a diamond. Probably a good thing texting wasn't around back when they were dating. But Julianna and Namiko — Her thought was cut short when Aunt Glori opened the front door.

"How's it coming? Did you get my voice mail?"

Di looked at her phone. "I saw that you called but didn't realize you left a message. What's up?"

"Just wondering when y'all planned to go to Julianna's performance. I was out and about and figured I'd stop in rather than waiting for your answer."

"Mitch and I are going on opening night. Friday is the night before the estate sale, and I expect to be too tired to go on Saturday after the sale. Is Thursday okay with you?"

Lyndee Rae joined them in the living room and greeted Aunt Glori. "Your daughter's play is this weekend? Do you think Paisley would enjoy it?"

"I'm sure she would," Di said, "especially if we arranged a meeting with Cinderella herself."

Lyndee Rae beamed. "She would love that. Oh, but we can't go on Thursday, and I do want to help with the sale."

Di tapped a finger on her lips. "They have a dress rehearsal tomorrow. Let me talk to Julianna and see if it would be okay for you to attend that. Might even be easier for her to come out and see Paisley then."

"That would be wonderful. Thank you."

"Okay then." Aunt Glori stepped toward the door. "I'll see you and Mitch on Thursday. Bye, Lyndee Rae. Enjoy the show."

―――――

At 3:30, Di mashed the cover onto a file box of nineteen-year-old tax returns and blew her bangs off her forehead. "I'm done."

Lyndee Rae appeared at the door of the bedroom. "Good, I'm ready for a break, too."

"No, I mean I've had enough." Di shoved the box into its space in the crowded closet. "We've looked through this whole house, every closet, cupboard, corner and cranny, and still no painting. I've spent way too much time on this. If Eva can see us, she'll have to be satisfied I did my best with what she gave me." Di pushed herself up from the floor and stretched her back and legs. "How's your room coming along?"

"Still working on that closet. Amazing how much stuff she packed into a six-by-three-foot space."

"And it's all junk." Di pointed to various items in her room. "My grade school papers, newspaper clippings, cards from birthdays and Christmases long gone. Ancient gift-wrapping paper. Cheap doodads and trinkets from her travels." Di threw her hands in the air. "Worthless, just like the things she expects me to pass on. Who's going to prize something that has no value whatsoever?"

"Are you forgetting about Paisley?" Lyndee Rae lifted one knee onto the bed and sat.

"That doll probably wouldn't sell for fifty cents. But to my daughter, she's priceless." She swept her hand across the quilt and played with one of the yarn ties. "Please don't take this wrong, Di, but worth isn't always measured in dollars and cents. Sometimes it's measured in the heart."

Di sank onto the bed. "That's rather profound."

"It's true. All those baubles and knick-knacks that seem trashy to you? To Eva, they represented memories of favorite places and good times. Those old school papers of yours? A reminder of you as her carefree little girl, before you became a grown-up woman with all kinds of responsibilities."

"Too busy to spend time with her." Here came the guilt.

Lyndee Rae touched her arm. "I'm not saying this to make you feel bad."

"I know." She didn't need any help for that. She could blame herself just fine.

A smile played around Lyndee Rae's mouth. "Now I have a story for you. Years ago, my uncle gave my aunt a lamp she'd been wanting. I think it was a Christmas gift. Later, after he died, that lamp fell over and broke all to pieces. Aunt Betty was terribly upset because to her, it represented my uncle's love. One day, she found a very similar one for sale and she bought it. Months later, she found another one and bought that too. Eventually she bought a third lamp, and a fourth one. All because she didn't want to be without a lamp that reminded her of Uncle Joe."

Di smirked. "At least they're useful and serve a purpose."

"Maybe, but do you know anyone who actually uses twenty-one lamps?"

"Twenty-one? All the same?"

Lyndee Rae shook her head. "No. It became an obsessive habit. The later ones had nothing in common with the original. But as an object, they reminded her of Uncle Joe. She put some in every room. In old age, her memory became unreliable, and she couldn't trust her mind to hold on to what was important to her. Those lamps helped her not to forget Uncle Joe." She shrugged. "Silly to us, but why else do we buy souvenirs when we travel? To make sure we don't forget our experiences."

Thoughts churned in Di's mind. Mother had always been sentimental. Too bad she hadn't lived long enough to explain the memories behind the items on her list. Aunt Glori knew what the doll meant to Eva, and the vase. Maybe she'd have some insight on the piano and the painting, too.

But would that be enough to help her find the painting? Or identify who might treasure all these things?

15

*Cinderella
Requests a special audience
with*

Miss Paisley Wagner

*Wednesday evening
immediately following the performance*

The cream-colored card, lettered in gold ink with elegant handwriting, brought a gasp from Lyndee Rae.
"Did you do this?"
"Not me," Di said. "Julianna. She can't wait to meet Paisley tonight." She tied a trash bag and hefted it toward the door.
"That's so sweet of her. Paisley will be thrilled." She slid the card into her purse, careful not to bend it or let the corners get crushed.

"Since it's dress rehearsal, the front entrance will be locked. You'll have to go around back and knock, and someone will let you in. Tell them you're Julianna's guest. She'll meet you and Paisley in the auditorium right after the play."

Lyndee Rae's eyes sparkled. "Paisley doesn't know yet. I didn't want to disappoint her if it didn't work out. But she'll be so excited, especially with a personal invitation. We'll stop and pick up some flowers for Julianna on the way."

"Oh, she'll love that. Thank you." Di carried the trash out to the bins, a pointless act considering the whole neighborhood would be in ruins in less than a week. But the house needed to look as clean as possible for Saturday, which might be difficult if the predicted rains occurred.

She glanced up at the sky. May was the rainiest month in central Texas, with storms possible this afternoon and continuing throughout the weekend. You'd never know it by that cloudless blue. With luck, any precipitation that fell on Saturday would hold off until late afternoon or evening.

Back inside the house, Di said, "I have someone coming to look at the piano this afternoon. As soon as that's done, I'm leaving so I can feed Julianna and send her off to the theater in time to dress and do her makeup."

"I'll probably take off early too, if that's all right. I need to tell Kurt our plans and have him make sure Paisley takes a nap this afternoon."

"Will he go with you to the play?"

"I hope so. It's not exactly his type of entertainment, but I'm pretty sure that if Paisley asks in her enchanting little voice, Daddy will jump through any hoop she wants."

Di checked her watch. Lyndee Rae had already gone home, and Lauren Todd should've been here thirty minutes ago. The wedding planner had changed her mind about the piano and asked to see it. Di juggled her keys in hand as a car stopped at the house.

Lauren ran breathless up to the door as Di opened it. "Thank goodness you're still here. I was afraid I might miss you. My wedding planning session ran long. This girl could not make decisions, and her poor fiancé was obviously bored out of his mind and couldn't care less."

Di put on a patient smile. "No problem. Wedding plans are big decisions." She indicated the piano. "I haven't had any other inquiries, so if you want it, it's yours. Only you'll need to move it out of here before Monday."

Lauren studied the piano. "Ooh, so soon?"

"You probably noticed the demolition going on a couple blocks away."

"Yeah, what's that about?"

"Redevelopment, or flipping the neighborhood." She used air quotes. "Next week, they start on this block."

"Hmm." Lauren chewed the inside of her cheek, her mouth pulled to one side as she examined the instrument. Sitting on the bench, she tapped a couple of dusty keys, then wiped her fingers on her pants.

Di grimaced. She whisked out a cloth rag and ran it over the keys. "Sorry. I should've wiped this down before you came." What kind of cleaning lady was she to overlook such an obvious task?

Lauren's fingers moved over the ivories in a melody Di didn't recognize. "When was the last time you had it tuned?"

"Years. Maybe a couple decades. My mother didn't play, so I doubt she ever tuned it after Dad passed." Di shifted her feet.

"I admire you being able to play from memory. My dad could do that. He tried to teach me, but apparently, I didn't get the musical gene."

Lauren nodded. "I'm not sure it can be brought completely back in tune." She stopped, lowered the cover over the keys, then ran her hand over the music stand, the top and the sides as if sizing up a horse. Check the teeth, the back, the legs....

"It's not in bad shape." Lauren stood and pushed in the bench. "How much do you want for it?"

"Mother specifically wanted it to go to someone who will love it."

Lauren bit her lip. "Hmm. Can't say I'm that crazy about it."

Di's heart sank. Further confirmation that this piano was worthless. "Maybe someone coming to our estate sale on Saturday will fall in love with it." She checked her watch. "I hate to rush you out, but my daughter has a dress rehearsal tonight and I need to get home."

"Oh, sure. I won't keep you. Is she in a play?"

"She's Cinderella in the children's theater performance." Di grabbed her purse and opened the door, ushering Lauren outside.

"How cool. Tell her to break a leg."

Di accompanied Lauren out to their cars. The sky had clouded over, and the air hung heavy and still. "What a change from this morning. Maybe we'll get some rain after all."

"I just hope it doesn't get nasty. We're under a tornado watch until later tonight." Lauren got into her car and lowered the window. "I'll let you know about the piano, but don't hold it for me if you find someone who loves it. Take care." She waved and drove off.

Di scanned the sky before pressing the ignition. Texas

weather could be so unpredictable. If any storms materialized, they might be small enough to rain on one neighborhood while another only a few blocks away remained dry. Or they could be a gully washer. Good thing she planned to hold the sale inside the house. No need to worry about furniture, appliances, or shoppers getting wet.

On the drive home, she made a mental note to post sale notices to local social media sites and the *Tribune-Herald* newspaper. Lyndee Rae could help her make up signs to place along the streets leading to the house. And she'd need to stop at the bank for some cash to make change.

Minutes later, she entered the kitchen and dropped her purse on the counter. Julianna stood at the stove, a grilled cheese sandwich sizzling in the frying pan.

"Sorry I'm late, honey. A client came by to look at the piano."

"It's okay. I don't really want a lot on my stomach. Kinda nervous. I'll eat more when I get home if I'm hungry." She turned the sandwich over and pressed it down against the skillet. Lifting the spatula, she flicked it back and forth. "I'm worried, Mom. What if I forget my lines?"

Di removed some fruit, cut veggies, and milk from the fridge. "I'm sure you'll do fine, sweetheart. You said them perfectly the last time we ran through them with you. And remember there'll be a prompter just off-stage if that happens." She handed Julianna a plate and set a glass of milk on the table.

"Will Paisley be there?"

"Yes. I think Lyndee Rae was as excited as Paisley will be. Your invitation was perfect."

"I can't wait to see her expression when I come out to meet her." Julianna bit into her sandwich. "Mom, what did we do with Grand Eva's class ring?"

"I put it in her jewelry box in my bureau. Why?" Sitting across from her, Di leaned on the table with crossed arms.

"David, the kid who plays the prince, is supposed to wear a big gold ring. He managed to misplace the one he had, so I wondered if we could use Grand Eva's." Her fingers tapped a continuous uneasy rhythm on the table.

"Can I trust him with it when he's already lost track of one?"

"I'll be responsible for it. I'll make sure he gives it to me whenever he's not wearing it for the show." Julianna took a drink and set her glass down.

Di frowned and fiddled with her necklace. "I don't know. I hate to risk losing it."

"Can we at least get it out and look at it, see if it would work?"

Di hesitated, then retrieved the box from her bedroom and opened it at the table. She pulled out the ring and slipped it onto her forefinger.

Julianna wiped the sandwich's light grease from her fingers and took hold of Di's hand, moving it this way and that to catch the light from the chandelier above the table. "See? It's big and gold and shiny, and it'll reflect the stage lighting perfectly. Especially if he wears it like that on his pointer finger. Please, Mom?" She smiled in such a pleading way.

Di gave in and removed the ring from her finger. "All right. But don't you dare lose it."

"I won't. I promise." Julianna slipped the ring onto her thumb and rotated it under the light.

Di picked up Julianna's plate and empty glass and rinsed them. A glance out the window revealed a darkening sky. Trees thrashed in a strong wind gust but so far, no raindrops tapped against the pane. She turned to Julianna. "Looks like it's going to storm. Maybe I should drive you over."

"But then you'd have to come back after the rehearsal. I've driven in rain before. I'll be fine."

"Are you sure?"

"Don't worry, Mom."

Worrying is what mothers do. But she never wanted to be one of those helicopter parents. "You'd better get going then. The rain might take you a little longer."

"Just need to brush my teeth and grab my backpack." Julianna jumped up from the table, stuffed the ring in her pocket, and hurried out.

Di checked her phone but found no weather alerts. A light patter of rain quickly intensified to a downpour that sent angry drops beating against the glass. Minutes later, it quit as quickly as it started. The wind calmed and late afternoon light shone through a break in the heavy clouds.

Julianna returned with her backpack slung over one shoulder. "Wish me luck."

"I think I'm supposed to say break a leg, right?" Di hugged her. "You'll be great tonight. Try to relax and have fun with it. Imagine Paisley out there and act like it's just for her." She kissed her forehead.

"I will. Thanks, Mom."

"Be careful driving. That storm may not be completely over yet."

"Okay." Julianna reached for the doorknob.

"Text me so I'll know you got there okay."

Julianna rolled her eyes on her way out the door. "Yes, Mother."

Di ignored the gesture. "Do you have the ring? Oh, right, it's in your pocket. Don't forget to greet Paisley afterward. Drive careful."

Maybe she should've gone with Lyndee Rae tonight to give Julianna moral support. Would she get nervous and flustered, forget her lines? What if she did? Wasn't that part of growing up—learning to overcome mistakes and hold on to your worth in humiliating circumstances?

Di watched until the car cleared the driveway. "Enjoy the ball, Cinderella. Make it home by midnight."

16

The next morning, Lyndee Rae carried Paisley into the house and settled her on the couch. The girl wore a princess outfit and held tight to Raggedy Ann. The blue around her lips appeared more pronounced. Or was that because her cheeks looked especially pale? Lyndee Rae adjusted a pillow, and Paisley rested her head on it.

Di squatted beside the sofa. "I hear you met someone special last night."

Paisley nodded, her voice almost a whisper. "Cinderella."

Julianna told her all about it when she came home from rehearsal, but Di looked forward to Paisley's account. "Was that fun?"

"Uh-huh. Her dress was pretty, the one she wore to the ball."

"I bet it was. What did you two talk about?"

"My dolly. She needs a new heart like me. Cinderella said her fairy godmother might find us both a new heart, but," she paused and seemed to catch her breath, "but I told her Jesus is already working on that. Maybe the fairy godmother could find me a dress like hers." The girl's chest rose with a deep breath, then she put her thumb in her mouth and closed her eyes.

Di glanced at Lyndee Rae, whose wrinkled brow and the deep crease at the top of her nose wrapped Di's stomach in a rubber band.

Lyndee Rae covered Paisley with a light blanket. "You rest, sweetheart. I'll be right here if you need anything." She smoothed the hair from Paisley's face and the girl's eyes remained closed.

Di put an arm around Lyndee Rae's shoulders while they moved to the kitchen and spoke in hushed tones. "Was last night too much for her?"

Lyndee Rae chewed her thumbnail. "I don't know. It's hard to tell if it's that or the progression of the disease." She hugged herself and swallowed hard. "I didn't want to bring her, but I couldn't leave her either."

Di pulled her close and wrapped both arms around her. "You don't have to stay. If she's more comfortable at home, go. She's more important than anything you're doing here."

Lyndee Rae inhaled an uneven breath and blew it out. "Let's wait and see how she does. She went to bed later than usual and, with all the excitement, she had trouble falling asleep. Maybe she'll rally if she has more time to rest."

"Tell you what. I brought stuff to make signs for the sale. Why don't you work on those at the table where you can keep an eye on her?"

Lyndee Rae nodded and positioned herself where she could see Paisley. "Your daughter was wonderful, by the way. You'll love the show." She grabbed a fat marker and went to work on the signs.

Di snuck a peek at the child, so frail and innocent. Maybe it was good for Lyndee Rae to have something to do besides watching her daughter and worrying.

She tore out another trash bag and moved through each room in the house, collecting anything that wasn't destined for the sale. It rankled that the last item on Eva's list, the star painting, was still missing. It should've been with the Christmas decorations if it was a nativity scene. If it meant so much to Eva, why had Di never seen it? But then, she couldn't remember seeing the other things either besides the piano and that one time she saw Raggedy Ann.

Her phone jingled a call. "Hey, Scott. What's up?"

"Are you at Eva's?"

"Yes. Why?"

"I'm taking the bird up."

"The bird?"

"The helicopter. Mitch is here. You want to ride along?"

Di grinned. "I appreciate the offer, but no thanks."

"Y'sure? I can land a couple blocks away and pick you up."

"Nope."

"Why not?"

"Don't you remember how I panicked on the Ferris wheel? You had to peel my fingers off the safety bar."

Scott laughed. "I forgot about that. Trust me, this is perfectly safe."

"So was the Ferris wheel."

"You don't trust me?"

"I trust you. It's the machine that bothers me. And the height. Not the way I want to die."

"Ah, come on. You'll love the view once you get up there."

"Sorry, Scott. Mitch will love it, but not me. You two have fun."

He chuckled. "All right, creampuff, I'll let you off this time."

Creampuff? Really?

Di's heels drummed the floor.

Would Julianna remember her lines? Last night she'd sought to quell her daughter's nervousness with her own confidence. Tonight, it seemed she'd taken on the jitters herself. Di fanned her face with the program guide.

From their position in the center of the second tier, Mitch watched young children vie for front row seats with an amused smile on his face. In spite of it being a school night, the small, intimate theater filled quickly.

Aunt Glori kept up a steady stream of conversation. "Great view here. But with a theater this size, there really isn't a bad seat in the house. How was our girl today? Excited? Nervous?"

"Definitely excited, but not as nervous as last night. She said the dress rehearsal ran into a few hitches, but she thought they had everything worked out."

The lights blinked a two-minute warning.

Aunt Glori scanned the audience. "It's too bad Eva can't see this. She'd be so proud."

Di's heels stilled. A hollowness formed in her chest. Was Eva somehow watching tonight?

Aunt Glori interrupted her thoughts. "Are we all set for Saturday's estate sale?"

"Pretty much. Lyndee Rae and I will put signs out tomorrow along the busier streets and through the neighborhood directing people to the house. We also need to set out some of the sale items and arrange them in attractive groupings." She tried not to imagine the house being flattened in less than three days, but the thought always lurked in some shadowy part of her mind.

The theater lights dimmed. Stragglers scurried to find their seats, and Di squirmed to a more comfortable position. The curtains parted to reveal the ornery stepmother and stepsisters quarreling over who was most likely to catch the prince's attention.

A smattering of little girls applauded when Cinderella appeared in her tattered dress, her cheeks smeared with ash. Julianna looked beautiful and spoke her lines with confidence. Di reached for Mitch's hand, and he returned her squeeze.

Cinderella shrank back when the others mocked her appearance and her station in life, and Di's pulse ticked up a notch. Was she reacting to the snobbish attitudes and critical words aimed at her daughter? Or was she identifying with Cinderella—the cleaning woman with no status, the one always tidying up someone else's mess? She'd never before recognized herself as the young girl craving attention and validation, unable to break out from the shadow of a mother who drew the notice of people around her the way nectar attracts hummingbirds.

Oh, Eva never mistreated her, but Mother was completely unaware of her charismatic personality. How many times had she stood by Eva's side while someone spoke to her mother for several minutes, then left without ever acknowledging Di's presence. Not even with a glance. Dad once consoled her by confessing he too often went unnoticed while with Eva. Mother was oblivious to her own magnetism.

Di gave a slight shake of her head, ridding herself of the old wounds, at least for tonight. She lifted her chin, straightened in her seat, and smoothed the creases in her pants legs. Her hand crept up to take hold of her diamond necklace.

Julianna gave an award-worthy portrayal of Cinderella. Her appearance in her ball gown brought oohs and ahhs from the little girls in the audience and took Di's breath away as well. She glanced at Mitch who eyed his daughter with chin high and a satisfied smile.

When had their little girl turned into such a beautiful

young woman? She twirled and danced with the prince, her gown swishing and swirling around her feet. Her expression held such enchantment as she gazed at the prince, Di could almost believe Julianna really was in love. Wonder how Namiko felt seeing her like this.

A secret smile touched her own lips, recalling a long-ago prom when her face probably held that same expression. Those high school dances were nothing like this elegant ballroom waltz. Had they really considered all that twisting and gyrating romantic? Whatever. The memory of Scott lacing his fingers with hers and leading her out to the floor for a slow dance stayed vivid these many years since. Why? What was it about him that kept her cherishing those memories for so long?

The clock at the ball chimed midnight. Cinderella gathered her skirts and rushed from the stage. The curtains closed on the prince running after her, calling out to her.

Aunt Glori leaned over and whispered. "She's fantastic. She should consider acting as a profession."

Di offered a distracted agreement. Something niggled at her, playing hide and seek around the edges of her mind. She couldn't quite put her finger on it. What puzzle piece was she trying to find, and where did it fit?

The curtain opened once more with the prince trying to find the one foot that fit the glass slipper. Glass? Who in the world would want to walk, much less dance, in a shoe made of glass? No wonder Cinderella kicked it off as she left the ball.

At last, the prince arrived at her house where the stepmother had locked Cinderella in a room. But her pet mice slipped the key under the door. She escaped and ran outside, catching the prince before he left. The glass slipper fit perfectly to the consternation of her stepmother and stepsisters. Cinderella glowed in the certainty that she alone was fit for a prince.

A virtual spotlight flashed in Di's mind. That was it, the last puzzle piece. She had more in common with Cinderella than being a mere cleaning woman. Scott had been her prince, the reason she'd let him take up residence in a corner of her heart. Or so she'd always thought. Certainly, he was part of it, but what she'd been clinging to all these years wasn't Scott so much as the way he made her feel when they were dating.

He'd been a senior, a talented athlete, well-known, and liked by nearly everyone. She was an unknown sophomore, a nobody who blended into the scenery . . . until he asked her out. Suddenly, everyone knew who she was. No longer invisible, no longer eclipsed by her popular mother, Di felt valued, noticed. Scott had looked past all the other distractions, pretty faces and all, and convinced her she was worth his attention. For the first time in her life, she believed in her own self-worth. No wonder she'd clung to those memories for so long. And now, with the curtains closing, she could finally release them.

She stood, applauding the performance, and turned to Mitch. The glow that lit Cinderella's face now lit hers. She'd married her own prince, the only other man who could do what Scott did. Those old memories had lost their power over her.

17

A cannula delivered oxygen directly into Paisley's nose as she lay on the couch the next morning. Even with the increased gas, the blue hue of her skin and fingernails hadn't changed. Her thin arms kept a tight hold on Raggedy Ann.

Di couldn't help watching her while stapling signs around the metal frames.

"I'd like to get these out on the streets now where people will see them. We can work on the displays when I get back." Finished, she plucked jangling keys from her purse.

"Want me to drive?" Lyndee Rae gathered the prepared signs. "It'll go faster. You can jump out, stick them into the ground, and hop back in."

"What about . . . ?" Di shot a glance at Paisley.

"That's why I offered to drive. She'll be okay in her car seat. Let me load these up. I'll be right back." Moments later, Lyndee Rae returned and gathered Paisley in her arms. "We'll go for a little ride, okay? You can rest in your car seat." Paisley nodded and laid her head on her mother's shoulder. "Di, would you bring the oxygen canister?"

At the car, Di handed the apparatus over to Lyndee Rae. Checking the overcast sky, she said, "If it rains, these tagboard signs will be useless. I should've gotten more of the plastic ones." Her hair stuck to her neck in the humidity. She lifted it away and hand-fanned herself.

"Supposed to be a cool front coming through later. Kurt said there's a possibility of some rough weather. But they say that all the time and usually nothing happens." Lyndee Rae buckled Paisley in, then got behind the wheel and started the car.

Di posted several signs directing people through the deserted neighborhood. After several stops, she peered into the back seat while getting into the car. Paisley's eyes were closed, her mouth slightly open, her head leaning over to one side.

"She's still tired out from attending the play?" Di climbed into the car and tossed her head toward the back seat.

Lyndee Rae peered in the rearview mirror and frowned. "I think it's more than that. Call it mother's intuition but I have a strong feeling something's not right. Would you mind if I take a minute to see if I can get her an appointment with the doctor today? I hate to go through the weekend like this."

Di turned to study the frail little girl while Lyndee Rae talked with the medical office.

"They'll work her in late this afternoon," Lyndee Rae said a few minutes later. She tucked her phone away.

"I don't know how you do it." Di faced forward again. "I'd be a basket case."

Lyndee Rae shook her head. "If you were in my position, you'd find the strength to do whatever Julianna or Mitch needed."

"But you take everything as it comes, and you don't get

riled or anxious." Di pointed to the intersection ahead with a traffic light. "Stop up there."

Lyndee Rae pulled to the corner and Di climbed out of the car, pushed a sign's stakes into the ground, then climbed back in.

"So how do you do it? What's your secret?" Di pulled her seatbelt around her and clicked it in place.

"First, let me ask you a question," Lyndee Rae said, "What do you think of God and Jesus?"

"I go to church, so I guess I believe in them." Di named their place of worship.

"That's part of it, but it's deeper than that. Let me ask it another way. Are Jesus and God real to you? Or are they just some ancient stories in the Bible?"

Di indicated another stop, got out and stuck the sign in the ground, then got back in the car. "I never really thought about it. Eva and Dad always took me to church, so I guess I've always accepted that they're real."

The conversation continued in between stops.

"Has going to church and knowing the people in the Bible were real made any difference in your life, like in the way you live or the decisions you make?"

"Aside from being honest and trying to do the right thing? No, I guess not. Isn't that enough?"

Lyndee Rae nodded. "I used to think so. I grew up in Indonesia. My parents were missionaries there."

"How long did you live there?"

"We moved back to the States so I could attend high school here. But I learned about God and Jesus and all those Bible stories pretty much from the time I was born. I thought I had it all figured out, everything under control.

"Shortly after Paisley's birth, we sensed something was wrong. Finding out she had a defective heart and might not live long was overwhelming. I was a wreck. I called my parents, crying so hard I could barely get the words out. They prayed for us and encouraged me to read my Bible. Dad suggested a couple of places to start. Do you remember the story about the paralytic that couldn't get into the pool ahead of the other crippled people?"

Di searched her memory but came up empty. "Not exactly."

"There was a pool in Jerusalem where people with various physical disabilities sometimes got healed. At certain times, the water would ripple or move somehow, and all these crippled people would race to be the first one into the water. Supposedly, only the first one into the pool was healed. One man, a paralytic, had been there for thirty-eight years when Jesus walked through one day and told him to stand up, grab his mat, and walk."

She glanced at Di. "I'm sure you've heard the second story about Shadrach, Meshach and Abednego?"

"Thrown in the fiery furnace, right?"

"Yep. They told the king their God was powerful enough to save them, but even if he didn't, they would never bow in worship to anyone else."

Di scratched her temple. "How does that relate to Paisley's situation?"

"I couldn't see the connection either. Maybe the miraculous healing but does that really happen nowadays? And how does getting thrown into a furnace have anything to do with my daughter needing a heart transplant?

"One night worry kept me wide awake. So I got up and read more of John's gospel, hoping for some context to the pool story. Something I'd never noticed before is that almost everyone who came to Jesus needed healing of some kind, either for themselves or for loved ones. Like Paisley, they had a real, physical need and they were desperate for his help. If

Jesus said *okay, you're healed*, they had to decide whether to believe him and act on it, or not. Everyone who trusted and believed that he spoke the truth came away changed. Their life was different physically, emotionally, spiritually."

"That makes sense." Faith hadn't made that much difference in Di's life, but of course, she didn't have a physical need. "What about the three in the furnace?"

"They faced the opposite dilemma. Their decision to believe and honor God meant certain death rather than healing. But they still said that even if God doesn't come through for us, we choose to honor him as God anyway.

"That's when I realized I have a choice, too. I felt desperate and helpless with Paisley's diagnosis, something I had no control over. I had to decide if everything I'd been taught was going to make a difference in my life or not. If these are all fables, nice stories but no real substance, then I have nothing. Paisley could die and that's the end. No more. No meaning."

"That's depressing. And hopeless."

"Exactly. But if I believe that miracles do sometimes happen, that God does care, and he actively works for our good, then I have hope. I choose to believe God will heal her, whether by a miracle or through medical means. But even if he doesn't, it's not the end because Jesus promised us there is life after death. I will see her again."

Lyndee Rae parked on the street in front of Eva's house, but Di made no move to get out.

"But you still grieve. I've seen your tears."

"Oh sure. Jesus doesn't expect us to lock our emotions away. Even he wept when his friend Lazarus died. But what you see in me? That's the difference between taking all those Bible stories and the things we were taught and internalizing them, believing they're for you personally."

"I guess it never occurred to me that those ancient stories

could apply to us today," Di said. "They all seemed too fantastical to believe."

"I know. The thing is, there were a lot of other invalid people around that pool waiting for healing the day Jesus walked through. We know of only one who said, 'Okay, I'm going to trust this guy because what other choice do I have?' I've learned to trust that God is capable of accomplishing anything I ask. Maybe more importantly, I've decided to trust him even if the answer isn't what I'm hoping for."

Could Di trust like that, believing God was working for her good even when it didn't look that way? Would he really take notice of her? Or was she still being too much of a Cinderella to believe she was worthy of anyone's attention?

After lunch, Di and Lyndee Rae moved through each bedroom evaluating the arrangement and display of furniture, lamps, bed linens, and any other sale items. Di dragged a rag across every surface to ensure it was dust-free.

"You never found that painting on Eva's list?" Lyndee Rae moved a bedside lamp and stooped to make sure it was plugged in.

"No. I'm not going to worry about it. If she thought it was that important, she should've put it where I'd find it. We've got every other item she wrote down, even if I've only found takers for a couple of them."

Di looked to Paisley lying quietly on the bed with Raggedy Ann. Lyndee Rae's fear that something was wrong prompted them to keep her close, moving her along to each room they entered. She seemed so lethargic but was it the diseased heart or did she need a higher concentration of the oxygen being pumped into her lungs?

"Let's move on to the kitchen and living room," Di said.

Lyndee Rae picked up the oxygen canister and carried Paisley from the bed. Di straightened the quilt and pillows and closed the door on her way out.

"Wow, it's gotten windy." Lyndee Rae stood with Paisley in front of the picture window. They watched the movement of the tree branches and loose debris blowing across the yard.

"Looks like the cool front has arrived." Di pointed to a corner of the living room. "Should we group all the lamps over there or leave them where they are?"

Lyndee Rae turned and looked about the room. "They look better where they are. What about the artwork on the walls? Leave it all there?" She sat Paisley in Eva's recliner and positioned the oxygen out of the way beside her.

"I think they show better that way, don't you? Although I don't know how many people coming to an estate sale will be interested in expensive art. I may have to take them to my house and find someplace to sell them."

"The library maybe?"

"Or a medical or business office. I wonder if Aunt Glori could use them for staging houses."

A deep, rolling rumble rattled the windows.

"Thunder, Mommy." Paisley snuggled with her doll into Eva's recliner. She lurched back to set it rocking then put her thumb in her mouth.

Lyndee Rae smiled at her. "Sounds like we'll get a little storm." She turned to Di. "Do you want to move any of this furniture?"

Di studied the room and muttered to herself. "I should've asked Aunt Glori to stage the house." Out loud, she said, "I must be getting tired. Let's leave everything where it is. If someone likes it, they'll make an offer no matter what position it's in."

"Were you going to have any signs about making an offer? I think people will expect to see prices on things."

"Good point. Would you rather work on signs or set out the kitchen appliances?" Di thumbed toward the kitchen.

"I'll do the signs. One for each room and maybe one for the front door?"

"Perfect."

Minutes later, a siren sounded.

Paisley's thumb popped out of her mouth. She jerked upright, eyes wide. "Mommy? What's that?"

Almost immediately, alarms blared from the phones. Di checked. Tornado warning. The storm could be in another part of town, but looking up, she saw her own concern mirrored in Lyndee Rae's expression.

The window now showed horizontal sheets of rain. Wind whipped the trees first one way, then the other. Her phone jingled, and she answered a call from Mitch.

"Where are you?" he demanded.

"At Eva's, getting things set up."

The lights flickered and went out.

"Anyone with you?"

"Lyndee Rae and Paisley."

"Y'all need to take cover now. They're tracking a tornado on the ground—"

Lightning lit the room. An immediate thunderclap. The house shuddered. Screaming, Paisley held her arms out to Lyndee Rae. Her mother grabbed her from the recliner.

Cr-ra-ack! A large bough broke from the tree, hurtled through the window to the spot where Paisley had been sitting. Lyndee Rae shielded her from the glass shards, their cries barely heard over the howling wind and snapping branches.

"The bathroom! Into the bathroom." Di strained against

the gale blowing through the open window, pelting them with dirt and debris. Paisley clung to her mother, crying and shrieking.

"Hang on," Lyndee Rae shouted. She tugged on the tubing to retrieve the oxygen canister only to find a sharp branch had severed it.

"Leave it," Di hollered. "Get into the bathroom. I'll grab it." Di wrestled the cylinder from under the branch and carried it into the small bathroom. She fumbled for the flashlight on her phone. How had she managed to hold onto it? She forced the door shut against the wind and locked it, cutting but not eliminating the wind noise that rivaled a jet taking off.

"You two get in the tub." Di held out the broken end of tubing. "Will it work to hold this to her nose?"

After climbing into the tub, Lyndee Rae removed the cannula and held the oxygen tube just inside Paisley's nostril. Hugging her daughter tight, she rested her head on Paisley's and settled back against the tub.

Paisley whined and covered her ears. "Mommy, my ears hurt." She shivered and snuggled against her mother. "I'm cold."

The temperature must have dropped ten degrees. The house trembled in the onslaught of wind, and Di fought a wave of disorienting dizziness before snatching the few towels and linens left in the cabinet. She tossed them to Lyndee Rae. "Here, cover up with these."

"What about you?"

"I've got one." She wrapped the bath towel around her shoulders and stepped into the other end of the tub, scrunching herself down to allow mother and daughter as much space as possible. Simply taking a breath became difficult amid the pressure, the roaring wind, and the clatter of debris that must mean certain destruction. If *she* was having trouble breathing—

"I'm scared." The storm nearly drowned out Paisley's small, frightened voice. "Mom-mee." Crawling up Lyndee Rae as if she were climbing a tree to escape a wild animal, she wrapped herself against her mother.

"It's okay to be scared. Do you remember what we do when we're afraid?"

"'When I am afraid, I will trust in the Lord,'" Paisley recited in short, breathy syllables.

"Why do we trust him?"

"I don't know," she whined. Her little body shook all over.

"Because 'he alone makes me dwell in safety.' And remember what Jesus did for his disciples when they were out in a boat and afraid of drowning?"

"He told the wind to be quiet," she raised her index finger as if to scold, then flattened her palm, "and he told the waves to stop." Her voice faltered at the end. She closed her eyes, and her hold relaxed ever so slightly.

Lyndee Rae touched Paisley's neck, searching until she found what she needed. She appeared to count, then closed her eyes. "Her pulse is weak."

Closing her eyes, she prayed out loud. "Jesus, save us. Calm this storm and protect us. Please keep Paisley in the palm of your hand. You're my only hope, Lord. I beg you, please."

Our only hope. For Paisley. For her and Lyndee Rae. One gust of wind, one fallen tree is all it would take. Could she trust God to save them? What other hope did she have?

Something crashed above them, sending bits of plaster and dust raining down on them.

Di covered Lyndee Rae's hand with hers and bowed her head.

18

Di's phone lit up with a text from Mitch. She sent a reply that they were safe for the moment. She'd let him know more later.

"I left my phone out there." Lyndee Rae jerked her head toward the bathroom door. "Would you mind letting Kurt know we're okay? He's probably worried sick."

"Of course. What's his cell number?" Di typed it into a text address box, hit the voice button and held her cell up for Lyndee Rae to speak her message. When she finished, Di pressed Send.

Lyndee Rae squirmed to a more comfortable position, if there was such a thing in a dry tub. "Thanks. Let's hope it goes through."

"It should. Mitch's did."

Lyndee Rae gazed up at the ceiling for several moments. "Does it sound like the wind might be dying down?"

Di listened. "I think so. Maybe it'll be over soon."

Lyndee Rae exhaled, closed her eyes, and murmured,

"Thank you, Jesus." Paisley still slept, her limp form resting on her mother.

"Is she okay?" Di asked.

Lyndee Rae again felt for a pulse. "About the same. Think we'll make it to our appointment this afternoon? I hope the doctor's office wasn't affected."

Di shrugged. She imagined trees and limbs down. Did she even dare hope their cars escaped damage and they'd be able to get home?

Twenty minutes later, the wind made no further sound. Di clambered out of the tub onto the floor, her knees and hips stiff from being cramped in a small space for so long. She put her ear to the door. A breeze flowed around her ankles. She unlocked the bathroom door, opened it cautiously, and peeked outside.

Drawing in a sharp breath, she covered her mouth. "Oh, my—"

Had she been transported to a war zone? A heavy tree trunk lay mere yards from where she stood, in place of the kitchen and dining room. Mangled gutters, a street sign, and torn shingles littered its branches. Other trees had been stripped of their new leaves and looked exhausted from Mother Nature's recent attack. Lyndee Rae's car sat upside-down in the street while her own car lay crushed beneath another tree. Leftover raindrops spattered her arms, and she breathed in the pungent odor of splintered wood, gasoline, and wet earth.

Lyndee Rae made a noise behind her. "Help me up."

Di turned and took Paisley into her arms. The girl didn't stir. Lyndee Rae hoisted herself from the tub and went to the door.

"Dear God," she said, stepping outside. "There's nothing left." She turned to Di, dazed, then looked back at the destruction and whispered, her voice filled with awe. "Thank you, Lord."

Di frowned. "For what?"

"Come see." Stepping back into the bathroom, Lyndee Rae held out her hands. "I can take her now."

One of Paisley's slender arms hung slack at Di's shoulder, but she hugged the child close before giving her back to her mother. She followed Lyndee Rae through the doorway. A few steps out, she halted, her breath frozen in her lungs. Besides the kitchen and dining area, most of the living room and bedrooms were torn away, their exposed walls left ragged. Only the bathroom survived intact. She gave a slow, disbelieving shake of her head. "How—?"

"I think you know the answer to that." Holding the severed tubing to Paisley's petite nose, Lyndee Rae observed their surroundings. "The question now is how will we get out of here? I'm really worried about Paisley." Her fingers searched for a pulse.

Di picked her way out to the street, slipping in mud, her shoes filling with water from the puddles. Downed trees, branches, and debris clogged the roadways in every direction. Here and there a power line sagged dangerously close to the ground. One of Eva's Christmas ornaments dangled from a bent streetlamp that leaned at a precarious angle. Clouds still billowed about the sky, but here and there patches of blue shone through.

"Diamond?" Lyndee Rae's voice shook. "Call 911."

Di pressed the emergency numbers then navigated the tornado's obstacle course to reach them.

"I can't wake her, and her pulse has become erratic." Lyndee Rae glanced around them. "And who knows where my phone is."

While waiting for her call to be answered, Di touched

Paisley's sweet face. Her skin felt cold and clammy. The call rang several times, the dispatchers likely overwhelmed with tornado issues. But this was a matter of life and death. She repositioned the phone to her ear and shouted.

"Someone answer the phone!"

As if on command, the operator picked up. "What is your emergency?"

"I have a child who may be going into heart failure." Di pressed the speaker option and held the phone so Lyndee Rae could talk.

"My daughter's not responding and has an erratic heartbeat. She's four and is on the list for a heart transplant."

"What is your location?"

Di filled in with the address. "An ambulance may not be able to get to us. The tornado went through here, and every street I see is blocked."

Unhurried, the operator asked more questions about Paisley's condition. "How close do you think you are to an open street?"

With little patience left, Di turned a full circle, looking for any possible route. "I don't see—" Something black and yellow in the distance caught her attention. Was that the roof of one of Scott's machines? If it wasn't damaged, he could clear a path for the ambulance. He might be able to get through on foot. "I know someone who can make a way out for us. I'm going to call him."

"Wait—"

Di cut off the operator and punched in Scott's number, then panicked. Had she hung up on the 911 operator after waiting so long to connect?

Lyndee Rae turned away, cradling Paisley in her arms, her head bowed.

Scott answered before she even heard it ring. "Diamond, where are you? Are you all right?"

"I'm at Eva's. I'm fine but my friend's little girl may be going into heart failure, and we're stranded. The ambulance can't get through. Is there any way you could get here and use your equipment to clear a path?"

"I'll do better than that. I was taking the bird up to look at the damage. I'll get as close as I can and transport them to the hospital."

"Is that safe so soon after the storm?"

"I've flown in worse conditions than this. I'll be there in a few minutes. Watch for me."

Di's shoes squished as she made her way through the rubble to deliver the news to Lyndee Rae. "Are you comfortable flying like that?"

"I'll do anything that gets her to a hospital." Her voice shook. "Would you call Kurt? See if he can meet us there."

Minutes after Di alerted Kurt, a soft beating of the air announced the helicopter's approach. Scott flew in a wide circle before coming near enough to hold up two fingers and point away from the house.

"I think that means two blocks," Di said. "Probably easier to land in an area they've already cleared. Go ahead. I'll be right behind you with the oxygen."

They wound through a maze of debris to where the helicopter hovered. Without the houses and lawns that used to be there, the whole block was a mud pit. An excavator lay on its side against a bulldozer. Demolition materials were strewn about, and the copter's downwash flung muddy water and grit that stung their eyes and arms.

Lyndee Rae turned her back and loosely covered Paisley's head with the towel that had somehow managed to stay wrapped around the girl's shoulders.

The helicopter swung away to a section of the street that held the least rubble, lifted, turned, and lowered again, giving them access to the passenger side. Scott motioned for them to approach.

Di looked at Lyndee Rae, squinting against the whirling chaff. She received a single brief nod.

"Let's go." She tucked her arm under Lyndee Rae's and they made their way to the helicopter. Off balance in the downwash, Lyndee Rae slipped in the slick clay mud that caked onto their shoes. Di barely kept them both upright. The racket was deafening. First the tornado, now the helicopter.

Lyndee Rae handed Paisley to her. "Let me get in first and then I'll take her."

Di took the child onto her shoulder, adjusting the towel to cover her head but not interfere with her breathing. Was she still breathing? Di's heart plummeted. She checked for a pulse. There. Weak, but as long as her heart was beating, Di reasoned, she must be breathing however shallow.

With Di's steadying hand, Lyndee Rae balanced on the skid, her fingers seeking the door latch. It opened under her pressure, but the door unexpectedly swung into her, knocking her back to the ground. She hopped onto the skid once more, gripped the door frame and pulled herself into the tight confines of the back seat.

Di stepped close and prepared to transfer Paisley.

Scott shouted above the noise. "Strap yourself in first."

Lyndee Rae pulled the harness across her body and clicked it into place, then leaned out and took Paisley.

Di lifted the oxygen canister, setting it on the floor between Lyndee Rae's knees, then closed the door, backed up, and signaled Scott to lift off. He gestured for her to get in, but she shook her head.

The helicopter rose, swung around, and settled again. Scott

pulled the headset off one ear and opened his door. "Diamond, there's no other way out. If I have to, I'll shut this bird down and personally strap you in. But I'm not leaving without you."

Di rubbed her sweaty hands on her pants. She couldn't stop her heart from racing at the thought of flying in the helicopter. Her knees went weak. She was costing them precious minutes to get Paisley to the hospital. If the child died because of her, she'd never forgive herself.

She took a step forward, her legs threatening to collapse. Bile crawled up her throat. Her chest tightened, making breathing difficult.

Paisley.

If she had to crawl to that awful flying machine and keep her eyes closed the whole time they were in the air, she'd do it. For Paisley.

Di swallowed hard as the helicopter lifted and the ground fell away, leaving behind the storm's chaos. At least she wasn't in the front seat with a panoramic view in front of her. But still her nausea rose with the altitude. The last thing she wanted was to vomit all over Scott's helicopter, but there wasn't even a window to open. No, that wouldn't help anyway. She shuddered at the thought of hanging out an open window with nothing between her and the ground far below.

The copter bobbed and swayed, sensitive to the air currents. She stiffened and her hands gripped the seat until her fingertips turned numb. She leaned her head back against the seat and closed her eyes. Inhale. Hold it. Exhale. Repeat.

Lyndee Rae's hand covered hers. Di turned her head sideways and forced her eyes open. This wasn't about her. This was for Paisley.

The constant chuffing of the helicopter made conversation difficult, but the calm encouragement in Lyndee Rae's eyes helped slow her heartbeat from a gallop to a trot. She traded her vise-grip on the seat for her friend's hand and reached her other hand to Paisley's frail body.

Then a glimpse beyond the confines of the copter sent her stomach into her throat again. She closed her eyes. Inhale. Exhale. She should text Mitch, but that would require opening her eyes. And letting go of the seat. Inhale. Exhale.

Scott shouted over the helicopter's noise. "Which hospital?" Lyndee Rae responded, and Scott explained, "Storm-related injuries will likely keep their helipad busy. If I can't get permission to land there, we'll try a parking lot or a lawn. I'll alert them to have a transport ready for you."

"Thank you."

"Diamond," Scott said, "you still with us?"

She nodded, keeping her eyes closed, then realized he couldn't see her sitting behind him. "Barely."

He chuckled. "Hang in there. We'll be on the ground before you know it."

Not soon enough. For Paisley or her.

19

"Thank God, we made it."

Di uttered her two most sincere prayers within ten minutes of each other—first when Paisley was taken into the hospital still breathing, and second when the helicopter finally set down for good in a grassy area near the hospital. They'd been allowed to use the hospital's helipad only to unload the child and Lyndee Rae. Air traffic control then directed Scott to the undeveloped field next to the hospital.

He cut the engine, checked the controls, and pulled the rotor brake. The overhead blades slowed their spinning, and he hopped out to open Di's door.

Her dizziness subsided in sync with the rotors, but he still pried her hand from its grip on the seat. Her wobbly legs nearly gave out. Not that she wouldn't love to kiss the solid ground, but Scott held her up, his lips curving into an amused grin.

She gave him an evil side eye and jerked her arm from his grasp. "You wouldn't be laughing if I hadn't kept my lunch from spewing all over your pretty helicopter."

His grin lost its humor. "Diamond, I saw the wreckage on my way in. You would've had to hack and climb your way out." He started toward the hospital.

"You're leaving the helicopter here? Is that okay?" She took a few shaky steps and gradually regained her balance.

"For now. It's locked."

"You're going inside?"

Scott stopped. "Did you think I'd just drop y'all off and leave? I'm not that callous."

His hand cupped her elbow, and he guided her toward the hospital. "Besides," he muttered, "someone has to make sure you stay upright."

Once again, she pulled away from him and took off at a march across the field to the emergency room entrance.

Casualties from the tornado crowded the waiting room. An elderly woman with a streak of blood down the side of her face stared at the floor, and a boy with scratches and scrapes all over held one arm close to his body.

Di checked with the desk. "My friend's little girl just came in unconscious with an irregular heartbeat. Would they be here or ICU or where?"

The receptionist squinted at her computer screen. "What's the last name?"

"Wagner. The daughter's name is Paisley. We brought them in." She indicated Scott and herself. "Is it possible for us to go back there with her?"

"Umm, let me check." She got up and disappeared into the back. A minute later, she returned, unlocked the door, and beckoned them in. "She wants you both to come back but you'll have to stay in the hall. There's a lot going on."

Di and Scott followed her to an actual room where Paisley lay with an oxygen mask covering the lower half of her pallid face. An IV snaked into a vein in her hand and electrodes on her chest gave a continual readout of her heartbeat. Di noticed it was still irregular. Medical personnel crowded the room, drawing blood, checking respiration, administering medicine, and monitoring every detail.

Di folded her friend into a hug.

Lyndee Rae blinked rapidly and reached out to Scott. "I can't thank you enough for what you did."

Scott sandwiched her hand in both of his. "Glad I could help. Has the doctor been in yet?"

"Just the ER doc. The pediatric cardiologist is on his way." Lyndee Rae crossed her arms in a self-hug.

"Kurt's not here yet?" Di asked.

Lyndee Rae shook her head.

"Do you want to call him?"

"Yes, please."

Di pulled up Kurt's number and handed the phone to her, then nudged Scott farther down the hall to allow her some privacy.

"What about Mitch? Do you need to call him?" Scott pulled up Mitch's number and offered his phone.

She accepted it and when Mitch answered, she recounted the events of the last hour. "I'm at the hospital now with Lyndee Rae and Paisley. And Scott."

"I'm on my way." A door slammed on Mitch's end of the call. "Aunt Glori will be glad to know you're okay. She's been calling every five minutes."

"Is she all right? What about Julianna?" Paisley and the crisis at hand had temporarily swept everyone else from Di's mind.

"Aunt Glori is fine. Cinderella is here with me. We'll be there soon."

She handed the phone back to Scott. "Thanks."

"Everyone okay?"

She nodded and glanced toward the waiting room door as it opened. Kurt stepped through, and she raised her hand in the air. "Right here, Kurt."

He left the nurse escort behind and rushed toward Lyndee Rae, who handed Di her phone. Arm in arm, Kurt and Lyndee Rae squeezed in between the nurses and technicians and stood at the foot of Paisley's bed.

Di tapped her friend on the shoulder. "We'll go wait in the lobby."

"No, don't go." Lyndee Rae glanced at Paisley's motionless figure, then turned her husband toward them. "Kurt, you know Di, but this"—she reached for Scott's hand—"is the helicopter pilot that brought us here." She blushed. "And I didn't even think to get your name. I'm so sorry."

"You've had more important things to worry about." Scott shook hands with Kurt. "Scott Jones. Glad I could help. I hope your little girl pulls through."

A whimper from the bed turned everyone's attention toward Paisley. Her eyes were open, and the medical team parted to allow Lyndee Rae and Kurt on either side of the bed.

"I'm here, sweetheart." Lyndee Rae squeezed her daughter's hand and kissed it.

The child's gaze swung to Kurt. He leaned over and kissed her forehead. "Hi, baby."

"Daddy." The mask muffled her words, but her little hand with the IV touched Kurt's chin. She stared at the IV a moment, then looked at Di and pointed at Scott. "Who's that?"

Lyndee Rae covered her hand with her own and gently curled the tiny finger inward. "Mr. Jones is the nice man who brought you to the hospital."

Paisley gazed about the room, as if finally noticing where she was. "Mommy, where's my dolly?"

Di's mouth fell open. "I don't remember seeing it ..."

Lyndee Rae's forehead wrinkled. She chewed the corner of her lip. "We didn't have it in the bathroom. She must have dropped it when the thunder scared us, and I grabbed her."

Di's heart sank. Anything that had been in the living room was gone by now, picked up and carried away like Dorothy to the land of Oz.

Lyndee Rae leaned toward Paisley. "We'll have to look for her. Do you remember that big loud thunder that made us jump?"

Paisley's face crumpled into tears. "I want my dolly."

"We'll try to find her, honey," Kurt assured her. "If we can't, Daddy will take you to pick out a brand new one. Would you like that?"

Paisley shook her head, adamant. "I want *my* doll." No sooner were the words out of her mouth than her eyes rolled back in her head, her eyelids closed, and her body went limp.

The monitor's alarm went off and the medical team rushed in from every direction. Shouting orders. Pushing Lyndee Rae and Kurt out of the way. A nurse hustled them all away, herding them back up the hall to the waiting room.

"I'm sorry to have to do this," she said. "We'll update you as soon as possible." She retreated behind the locked door to the exam rooms.

Lyndee Rae covered her mouth and cried softly into Kurt's shoulder.

Di stared unseeing at the closed door, her fingers worrying the diamond on her necklace. Her throat tightened, as did the knot in her stomach.

Nearby, Scott rubbed his beard, scratched his neck, and finally dug his hands into his pockets.

A familiar voice called, "Diamond!"

Relief infused Mitch's cry as he waved and hurried toward her.

Julianna ran into her arms and buried her face in Di's shoulder. "Mom. I'm so glad you're safe. We were so worried."

Mitch spread his arms around them both, and Di breathed deep the comforting scent of his aftershave mingled with Julianna's coconut shampoo.

Moments later, he released them and greeted Scott. Seeing Kurt and Lyndee Rae, he asked, "What's happened?"

"Paisley... the monitor..." Di choked on the words.

Scott explained, speaking just above a whisper. "The heart monitor alarm went off and they kicked us out. Happened just before you got here."

Lyndee Rae turned toward them, dabbing her eyes with a tissue. What little makeup she wore formed dark splotches high on her cheeks.

"Di," she said, "y'all really don't need to stay. We'll be okay."

Di flung her arm around her friend's shoulders. "No way I'm leaving you alone now. Are your parents nearby?"

She shook her head. "They're back on the mission field. And Kurt's parents are on a cruise. They'll be back in a few days." Dabbing her eyes again, Lyndee Rae's voice rose higher in pitch. "I only hope she makes it that long."

"Can we pray?" Kurt's voice trembled as he held his arms out. "Y'all are welcome to join us if you'd like."

Di leaned her head against Lyndee Rae's. Mitch and Julianna moved to form a circle.

"Come on, Scott." Kurt motioned him into the group. "We're not complete without you."

Scott joined them, his arm extended around Kurt on one side and Julianna on the other. They all bowed their heads as Kurt prayed.

"Lord, we need your help. Thank you for doctors and nurses, and all who are helping Paisley right now. Give them the knowledge and wisdom to treat her. Thank you for Paisley. We commit her to your care. In our weakness, it's hard to trust you and not dictate to you the outcome we desire. But we pray for your mercy and grace—" his voice cracked. "Please spare Paisley's life and restore her to us." He paused then continued. "Nevertheless, not our will but yours be done in her life and in ours. Amen."

During the next hour, Di alternately paced the waiting room and held Lyndee Rae's hand. The promised updates told them little, other than they were still working on Paisley, which at least let them know she was alive. Di's best attempts to avoid thinking the worst weren't always successful, especially when questions pestered like flies. What was happening back there?

Dear God, please don't let it be the same outcome as it was for Eva.

At last, the door to the exam rooms opened and a nurse called for Lyndee Rae and Kurt. Her business-like expression gave no clue to Paisley's condition, but she spoke softly with the couple who nodded and followed her through the doorway.

Mitch and Scott continued their quiet conversation. Julianna concentrated on her phone. Di strode the length of the waiting room and back. Lyndee Rae hadn't broken into tears at the nurse's news. That at least seemed positive. She moistened her lips again and tugged on her necklace, while her thoughts skipped from Paisley and her doll to Lyndee Rae to the house.

The tornado had done a lot of Scott's job for him. All those hours she'd put in sorting and searching, and now she wouldn't even get the satisfaction of holding the estate sale or fulfilling Eva's last wish. Only three of the five items from her list remained after the tornado—the vase that Namiko was working on, Aunt Glori's necklace, and the piano. In her mind's eye, she saw the piano sitting undisturbed when they emerged from the bathroom, but so what? Who would want a piano that was in no shape to make music?

If the painting had been hidden somewhere in the house, it was no doubt ruined by now.

And Paisley's doll. The one thing out of them all that she was certain someone treasured—stolen by a tornado.

Lyndee Rae and Kurt returned to the waiting room, their expressions somber but not grief-stricken. They held hands as they came to stand in front of the others. Di hurried to Lyndee Rae's side.

"She's alive, thank the Lord." Kurt ran a hand through his short hair. "They're transferring her to the PICU in Austin. She's high enough on the transplant wait list that if a heart becomes available, the doctors there can do the operation." He gave a deep sigh. "I'd like to pray for a donor, but that means someone else will lose their child. I-I can't do that." His voice broke.

"It's in God's hands." Lyndee Rae sniffed and slipped her arm around his back, closing any gap between them. "Anyway, y'all can go home now. We can't thank you enough for keeping watch with us. We'll pack up a few things. Kurt will drive down to Austin, and I'll accompany Paisley on the transport." She looked at Di. "Guess I won't be helping you clean up the mess."

Di shook her head. "Don't even think about it." She paused. "Actually, I believe I'll leave all that to Scott. It was going to be his mess anyway."

Scott raised his eyebrow.

"Thank you again, sir." Kurt shook his hand. "Our little girl might not be alive right now if you hadn't come to the rescue. I'll make sure you get some recognition for this."

Scott held his palm up. "Not at all necessary."

Kurt took out his wallet. "At least let me pay for your fuel. I'm sure it's not cheap."

Scott pushed his hands away. "No, please. It's an honor to have been of help."

After all the goodbyes were said, Scott walked out with Di, Mitch, and Julianna.

"What doll was the little girl so upset about?" he asked as soon as they were out of earshot.

Di explained Paisley's attachment to the Raggedy Ann doll. "I'm sure the storm picked it up and carried it somewhere else."

"Maybe I can do a flyover tomorrow and see if I can spot it anywhere."

Mitch bid Scott goodnight, and he and Julianna continued to the car.

"I'll be right there, hon," Di called, stopping beneath one of the porte cochere's bright lights. She turned to Scott. "I appreciate you coming to get us, even if I wasn't the most grateful passenger."

He grinned, then clasped his hands behind his neck and stretched his shoulders. "Thanks for letting me hang around. I hope I didn't intrude."

"Not at all, though I was kind of surprised. I didn't quite take you for that kind of guy."

"What kind is that?"

Di shrugged and pondered how to keep her foot out of her mouth. "You said you prefer being with your crew, so I didn't picture you being comfortable in such a personal and emotional situation."

"It was definitely outside my comfort zone." He gazed at her briefly, as if studying her, then raised his eyes to something off in the distance. "What I saw tonight—it's not the kind of thing I've experienced very often. The bond between you and Lyndee Rae, between her and Kurt, you and Mitch. Even Julianna wanting to be part of it." He scuffed the toe of his boot against the ground. "I'm thinking maybe I've been wrong, that my attitude toward close relationships needs some adjustment."

He swept his gaze back to her, his eyes softening. "Don't take this the wrong way. I'm not trying to come on to you." He scuffed his toe again. "You were good for me back when we dated, when things were so chaotic at home. Thank you."

Di smiled, aware that the old butterflies had finally flown the coop. "You're a good man, Scott. I'm willing to bet that lady friend of yours would be happy to have you resting your feet on her coffee table more often, maybe even permanently."

He grinned, tapped his brim in salute, and sauntered toward his helicopter.

20

In sharp contrast to the tornado's turmoil three days earlier, Monday dawned with brilliant sunlight against an azure sky. Di stared out her office window and struggled to get her mind back into work mode. She'd spent three weeks focusing on Eva's house and all that went with it. Her employees had kept the company operating as usual, and for that she was grateful. But she needed to get back to running the business.

Her office phone rang, and she picked it up on the second ring.

"Hey, Di. It's Lauren Todd. Do you still have that old piano?"

Now she wants it?

"I do, but the house took a direct hit from the tornado. I'm afraid the piano is in worse shape than when you saw it."

"Oh, no. I'm so sorry. Was there a lot of damage?"

"Not much left of the house. The piano is still standing but with some gashes and a lot more scratches, and of course it was drenched with rain. I doubt it'll be any good for producing music."

"That's not a problem. I wasn't planning to play it anyway. But is it too far gone that some sanding, elbow grease, and paint won't fix? I'd love it as a decoration piece for my venue."

"I guess you could fix it up. Your place didn't get any damage?"

"Some branches and a fence down, but we were lucky being in a different part of town. How soon can I come and get it?"

"As soon as they clear a path into the neighborhood."

"Wow, that bad, huh? Any idea how long that might be?"

"Not really, but I know someone who can probably do it quicker than the city crews. Do you have a way to transport it?"

"My dad has a truck and trailer."

"Okay, let me call my friend and I'll get back to you."

Two days later, Di drove to Eva's house in a new car, thanks to Mitch who lost no time replacing the one crushed in the storm. Scott's crew had cleared a path along the streets leading to the house, as well as the driveway. And he'd promised not to start demolition until Di took one last look around.

She waved to his workers on her way into the neighborhood, followed by Lauren and her dad. She parked on the street, while Lauren's dad backed the trailer up the driveway.

Di exited the car, noting the absence of the acrid odor from the aftermath of the tornado. The air smelled fresh and clean, and birds sang their songs as Di and Lauren stepped onto the concrete foundation.

"I can't believe this," Lauren said, gazing all around. "It's a wonder anything survived."

The tree trunk still lay diagonally across the former dining room and kitchen, its limbs and twigs littering what was left of the flooring. Plastic shopping bags snagged by the broken branches swayed in the gentle breeze. Loose papers tumbled over the ground, pushed along by the air currents.

"A friend and her little girl and I rode out the storm in here." Di pushed the bathroom door wide open and stood aside while Lauren peeked in. The memory of those eternal minutes sent a cold shiver down her back and she backed away from the door.

Lauren put her arm around Di and hugged her. "I'm amazed you survived this. God must have been watching out for you."

"I have no doubt about that." Di picked up a random cardboard box and checked its contents. Empty. She tossed it out of the way as Lauren's dad deposited two platform-moving dollies in front of the piano.

"You sure you want this, Lauren?" Her dad cocked his head and scowled.

She brushed away the twigs, broken two-by-fours, and tufts of insulation covering the instrument. After looking it over, she straightened, hands on hips.

"It's perfect, Dad. Just needs some sanding and a couple coats of white paint. I can't wait to start fixing it up." She turned to Di. "I won't need the bench, but I would like to offer you something for the piano."

Di gave a short laugh. "Are you kidding? I was afraid I'd have to pay to have it hauled to the dump. I'm surprised you like it so much."

"I know. When you first mentioned it, I couldn't imagine what in the world I'd do with a piano. But then I was looking on Pinterest and saw this great idea. I immediately thought of you. You'll have to come see it when I'm finished."

"I'd love to."

"Lauren," her dad said, "shove this dolly underneath when I lift the piano up. Then we'll do the other end."

"Let me help lift." Di found a handhold and they soon had the piano resting on the wheeled furniture dollies. The three of them guided and maneuvered it to the ramp and up onto the trailer. Lauren's dad secured it with straps.

Di waved as they drove away. One item off Eva's list. Now if she could only figure out why Eva had considered it such a treasure.

She wandered along the driveway back to the house, kicking at fragments of plywood and litter that might hide something more than shredded leaves or toads sheltering in the soft dirt. Even if she uncovered nothing of Eva's, there was always the possibility the storm had dropped photos or other items of value to someone else. Her gaze swept across the wreckage until her phone signaled a call.

Her breath caught in her throat. Daily text messages from Lyndee Rae kept her updated on Paisley's condition. Did a phone call mean bad news? She hesitated only a moment before answering.

"Is Paisley okay?"

"More than okay." Lyndee Rae's voice held a new timbre. "A heart became available. She just went into surgery. Please pray that it's successful."

Di pressed a hand to her own heart. "That's wonderful news. How's she been doing emotionally?"

"She still cries for Raggedy Ann. Have you had a chance to look?"

"I'm at the house now. One of my customers was thrilled to get the piano this morning. If I find the doll, I'll let you know right away."

"Thanks. And pray for the donor's family, too. They must be devastated to lose their little one."

"Of course." Di cut the call and slid the phone into her back pocket, saying a silent prayer for Paisley, for the doctors, the medical team, and the donor's family. "Lord, give them comfort and hope."

She opened her eyes and scanned her surroundings. If that doll was here, she'd find it. But where to start? She needed a system. When cleaning a house, she worked from the top down. Here? Start at the corners and work in.

She fit her hands into the work gloves she'd brought and walked along the curb. Sunlight glared off broken glass that lay scattered across the front yard. Good thing she thought to wear boots.

At the opposite corner, a door lay on the lawn, its etched glass miraculously still intact. Must have been someone's front door. She lifted it high enough to peek underneath but found nothing worth saving. She rounded the corner and walked along the side of the property. In the backyard of what used to be the neighbor's house, a baseball glove lay on its back as if waiting for a ball to drop into its pocket. She picked it up and found a name in black marker along the thumb. Later, she'd take a picture of it for the social media site where people posted items lost or found in the tornado. Maybe she'd take a photo of the door, too.

Di continued searching, stepping over limbs, looking under planks and moving in concentric squares until she arrived at the foundation. Besides the mitt, she'd found a framed wedding portrait from what looked like the 1970s, a baby's picture, and a pair of athletic shoes with the laces tied together. She deposited these on the corner of the house slab, then stared at what was left. The storm had swept most of it away, including Raggedy Ann it seemed.

She'd gladly purchase a new doll and even distress it a bit to make it look old. But Paisley would never be fooled. The white pinafore would be easy enough to fake, but matching the blue plaid underdress? Impossible.

Di moved toward the bathroom where they'd taken shelter. Maybe the child actually had the doll in there but she and Lyndee Rae simply didn't remember. The debris from atop the piano now lay against the baseboard, propped on top of newspapers, plastic bags and other detritus that had found safety from the wind behind the heavy instrument.

She kicked aside the rubble to scare away any snakes or critters hiding there. A square piece of metal leaned against the wall. Poking out from under it was a piece of blue fabric no bigger than the tip of her little finger. Di picked up the metal square and there lay Raggedy Ann gazing up at her with round, dark eyes, triangle nose, and thin, silly smile.

Di snatched her up, shook the dirt from her, and laughed. She pulled out her phone to call Lyndee Rae, but as she turned to leave, the laughter died in her throat. This was the end. She had no more reason to return to this neighborhood, this house, her childhood home. It was all gone—the memories, the people—Eva.

You've always been good at making things disappear.

This time she wasn't the one making them disappear. Di sank to the concrete foundation. "Mother, I'm so sorry I wasn't more understanding."

Her gaze swept slowly from the tangle of house remnants to the trash-strewn lawn in front of her to the broken trees and branches left by the storm. She did nothing to stop the tears rolling down her cheeks.

"If only I were good enough to make all this disappear. I'd set everything back in place like it was, including you, Eva. Please forgive me."

She looked down at Raggedy Ann in her lap, straightened the dirty pinafore and brushed some leaf fragments from her remaining hair. "Lyndee Rae was right. True worth is measured in the heart."

Later that afternoon, Aunt Glori set a cup of hot tea in front of Di and sat next to her, taking a sip from her own cup. She patted Di's hand. "You did your best for Eva. No one can fault you there. Personally, I'm glad the house and everything is over. You've been working so hard, I was worried about you. Grief takes a while, but you'll get through it."

Di tasted her tea. Her eyes stung from her earlier crying jag and her nose still hadn't fully cleared. "One of my clients who is opening a wedding venue took the piano."

"Well, that's appropriate."

"How?"

"Your dad was quite the romantic. He used to play love songs for Eva on that piano."

"Did he do that for you, too, when y'all were dating?"

Aunt Glori shook her head. "He tried, but I didn't appreciate that sort of thing. Too sappy. I think that's what drew Eva to him in the first place. A wedding venue. The perfect place for that old piano."

"It won't be making any music. I'm not sure what Lauren plans to do with it." Di fingered the doll lying on the table next to her.

"Are you going to fill in her hair before giving her back to the girl?" Aunt Glori topped off her cup with more hot water.

"Only if I can find a shade of orange that matches. I'll need your help with that if I do." Hand sewing may not be her best skill, but if she knew how to sew on a button, she should be able to mend the most important part. Shouldn't she?

She held the doll up. "I'm pretty sure Lyndee Rae laundered her when Paisley first found her. Do you think she'll survive another run through the washing machine?"

"Put her in a lingerie bag on delicate and I don't think you'll have a problem." Aunt Glori took a swallow of tea. "Misty Ballard called me."

"She's not selling her house, is she? After they remodeled the master bedroom for her dad? Oh, don't tell me something happened to him."

"No. She called because some relative of her husband's is moving to the area and looking for a house. She said you bailed her out at the last minute when her cleaning lady couldn't make it. Did you meet Ed when you were there?"

Di nodded. "Interesting man. You know him?"

"Of course. He dated Eva."

Di set her cup on the table. "He did?"

Aunt Glori smiled. "Eva already had her eye on your dad when she was going out with Ed. But I was dating Walter, so she had to wait her turn. Anyway, the draft took Ed out of the picture and that ended that. I'm glad he made it back from the war. So many of our boys didn't."

"Dad wasn't drafted?"

"He got a medical deferment. Some doctor thought he detected a heart murmur and sent him home. He'd never had a murmur before and never had one since. I guess the good Lord wanted him here."

Julianna popped into the kitchen from the garage with her school backpack. Di shared the news about Paisley's transplant, and Julianna pumped her arms in the air. "Yes! That makes me so happy. And you know what else makes me happy? The play is over, and I have the whole evening free. No more practices." She spread her arms and swooped around the table, then swung her backpack down and dug into a side pocket. "I've got Eva's ring, too, Mom."

Aunt Glori peered at the ring that Julianna set on the table. "Eva's ring?"

"Her class ring from the university. Actually, we figured it was probably Dad's because it's so big. The prince wore it in the play. But Dad inscribed her initials inside. See? Isn't that romantic?" Julianna held it up for Aunt Glori to inspect.

"Walter didn't have a class ring." Aunt Glori shook her head. "Neither did Eva. None of us did."

21

Eva's handwritten list lay on Di's bureau. A single line crossed through each of the words *piano* and *necklace*. Di added a question mark beside *vase*, unsure if Namiko intended to keep it as his art project or return it. She hadn't thought to ask. She'd love to see what he created with the broken pieces but wouldn't mind at all if he chose to keep it. *Rag doll* received a check mark. Di would deliver it to Paisley as soon as they moved her from PICU to a room on the general Pediatrics floor. For now, the doll sat on the bureau, still half bald, watching her with that wide-eyed, rosy-cheeked smile. She'd slid sideways on the smooth wood surface and now leaned against Eva's jewelry box.

Di straightened Ann enough to remove the class ring from the box. Had Eva forgotten she still had it, or had she purposely kept it as she did Aunt Glori's necklace? It didn't really matter now, but it needed to be returned to the proper owner. The ring wasn't on the list, but maybe this would make up for the painting she never found.

She closed the box and headed to Misty Ballard's house on this Friday afternoon, a week to the day after the tornado.

Misty opened the door and invited her in with a conspiratorial whisper. "I haven't even told Dad you're coming. He's going to be so happy." Misty's eyes sparkled, and she bunched her shoulders together. "Come on. He's watching his shows. He's as bad as Mother used to be with her soap operas." She chuckled and led the way to her father's suite.

"Dad?" She knocked on the door. "You've got company."

"Bring 'em in." Ed wheeled his chair around and squinted at Di, his face lighting with recognition. "You're back. Is Courtney sick again?"

"No, this is a personal visit." Di moved closer, clutching the ring in her hand.

"Oh?"

Misty pulled up a chair for Di, then settled on the bed.

Di sat, her knees almost touching Ed's, and leaned forward. "When I was here before, you mentioned losing your ring from the university. You told me you didn't really lose it so much as gave it away and it was never returned."

Ed nodded. "Yes, I remember."

"Would you tell me the name of the woman you gave the ring to?"

He shook his head. "That happened so long ago, it's not important."

"By any chance, was the young lady's name Eva Chapman?"

Ed jerked his head back. He stared at her, then leaned on his elbow to adjust his position in the wheelchair. "Did you know Eva?"

"She was my mother."

"You're Eva's daughter?" He looked at her, incredulous, then burst into a smile. "Of course. I see the resemblance now.

How 'bout that?" Ed sobered. "I'm sorry to hear she recently passed away. Your mother was an exceptional woman."

"Yes, she was."

Ed's lips turned up slightly and he shook his head. "Eva. I could tell she wasn't as serious about me as I was about her, but back then it was common for a young man to give his girl his class ring. I don't think this generation does that anymore." He turned a wistful gaze toward the ceiling. "More than anything, I wanted to know there was someone waiting for me back home. It's what motivated me through the long days and nights of the war. Gave me a reason to survive."

"I'm sorry it didn't work out," Di said.

"Don't be sorry. I'm not. If it had worked out, I wouldn't have married my lovely wife and I wouldn't have my daughter here to take care of me in my old age. I'd say that's worth far more than a ring." He winked at Misty.

"I agree, but I believe this belongs to you." Di took his hand and turned the palm up, then placed the ring in his hand.

Ed's eyes widened. He held it up and inspected the inside. "It is mine. There's my initials." He looked at Di in wonderment. "Wherever did you find it?" He slipped it over the knotty knuckles of his ring finger.

"It's a long story. I won't bore you with it, but since Mother is gone, I wanted to return the ring to you."

"Thank you, my dear." He reached for her hands and pulled her in for a brief hug. "You've made this old man very happy. Any time you want to entertain me with that story, I promise I won't get bored."

"That's the old piano?"

Di gaped at what had been a decrepit instrument destined for the dump.

"You like it?" Lauren held her hands out like Vanna White displaying a prize. Which it was. The cabinet, painted wedding white, beautifully set off the colorful plants and flowers sprouting from within. It stood in a protected alcove on the back patio of the house.

"I can't believe it's the same one." Di moved closer to inspect it. The top lid stood open forming a backdrop for ferns and coleus. Carolina jasmine spilled over the corners and sides, vines trailing to the ground. In place of the keyboard bright marigolds, dusty miller, and zinnias in white, hot pink, and burgundy composed a scene as lovely as the notes once played on the ivories.

Di read aloud the quotation scripted on the casement above the blooms. "Flowers silently whisper the secrets of the heart." She turned to Lauren. "I love that. Did you do the lettering?"

Lauren nodded. "The saying isn't original. I wish I could remember where I read it so I could put the author's name under it." She dug her hand among the flowers and brought out a square pot. "All of these are in containers so we can take them out and change them or let them get some sunshine in between wedding events. Gradually, I'll build up a stock of silk flowers too so we won't have to keep buying fresh ones. We also took out the soundboard and hammers and everything to make it lighter and easier to move."

"Brilliant." Di surveyed the rest of the yard that was in varying states of transition. "If you do the yard like you've done this piano, you'll have a gorgeous setting for weddings. Any idea how long before you can schedule your first event?"

"Already got one for the 4th of July, a little over a month. Of course, I had to bribe her." Lauren's cheeks turned pink. "Since

I couldn't show her the finished product and she'll be my first customer, I'm not charging her for use of the venue. I only asked her to post a review if she's satisfied with the results."

"So, you both have incentives to make it work."

"Exactly. And I can't thank you enough for the piano. I hope somehow your mother knows I consider it a treasure."

After lunch, Di watched the passing scenery as Mitch steered the car into traffic on I-35. He'd offered to drive her down to Austin to deliver the doll.

"Out for a Sunday drive. Does this mean we're turning into old folks?"

She smiled. "Not yet. We have a purpose for this road trip. You're not officially old until you're driving country roads on Sunday afternoon purely for entertainment."

He grinned. "That's good to know." Humming a Willie Nelson tune about being on the road again, he glanced at the doll in Di's lap. "Hard to believe anyone could have a heart transplant and be out of intensive care in little more than a week."

"Lyndee Rae said when Paisley was breathing on her own and off certain meds, the doctors thought she was stable enough to go to a regular room. But I expect she'll still be hooked up to an IV and maybe some other things."

"In that case, I may wait for you in the lobby."

"I expected that." Di stifled a grin.

As capable as Mitch was about everything else, he'd never been able to tolerate medical trauma. During Julianna's birth, he created quite a stir when he passed out cold, requiring as much attention from the medical team as she did. "I hope Paisley's awake while I'm there. Lyndee Rae says she sleeps a lot. I'd hate to miss her reaction to seeing the doll."

"That alone would be worth the whole trip." A moment later, he asked, "Have you heard from the university about Julianna's idea for a memorial garden?"

"They've agreed to it. The head of the art department and a couple of students are planning the mural. As soon as they figure out how long it will take to complete, we can set the date." Di adjusted the visor and pushed the AC down a notch.

"And you've got Eva's list all taken care of?"

"All except for the star painting. If I'd known why it was so important to her, I might have known what I was looking for and where to search for it." Di smoothed Raggedy Ann's dress and picked a spot of lint off her pinafore.

"Is there a connection between all the items she wrote down?"

"Maybe." Di played with her necklace. "The piano was Dad's. The necklace belonged to Aunt Glori, who said the doll was a gift to Eva from her sister. So, husband, sister, best friend—maybe those represent the three most important people to her? And the vase and painting were her talents?"

"That makes sense. Art was such a big part of her life. I could see her wanting someone to appreciate her work after she passed."

A heaviness settled over Di. If she were to make a similar list of important people, Julianna would be in the top two. Yet, she herself wasn't among those who meant the most to Eva. Was she that big a disappointment? Just a lowly cleaning woman, not even deserving of some junky symbol?

Di left Mitch in the hospital lobby and took the elevator to the Pediatric floor. Lyndee Rae had warned her not to expect a lot of emotion or excitement from Paisley. Some meds were meant to keep her calm, giving the heart and blood vessels time to heal.

Di knocked lightly on the door.

Lyndee Rae opened it and beamed. "Paisley, there's someone here to see you."

"No-oo," she whined. "Don't want to see them."

A patient smile spread across Lyndee Rae's face. "But she's brought something just for you, something you've been wanting." She gestured for Di to enter.

Paisley was shaking her head and frowning when Di entered, hiding the doll behind her back. A bandage collared the girl's neck from the respirator used in surgery. Several IV bags hung on a pole beside her bed and more than one monitor kept track of vital signs.

A chill raced through Di and for a moment, she envied Mitch down in the lobby. How could such a petite child have so many wires and tubes attached to her body? And this wasn't half of what she'd come out of surgery with. Di ached for the child. If she could, she'd gather Paisley into her arms and hold her close.

"Hi, sweetheart." Di moved to the side of the bed. "I found someone who really missed you. She insisted I bring her so she can help you get well again."

Paisley grew still as Di brought Raggedy Ann out from behind her back. The child's frown turned upside down and her eyes brightened. She reached for the doll with both hands and hugged it tightly, rocking side to side.

Lyndee Rae came up behind Di and embraced her shoulders. "Thank you so much. More than anything else, this should help her through all the recovery procedures."

"I'm so glad I found it. I almost missed it."

"Mommy, look!" Paisley had removed Raggedy Ann's pinafore and dress and held the doll up for inspection. "She has a new heart too. Just like me."

Lyndee Rae sucked in a breath. "Look at that. I bet that's where she was all this time you were missing her. She was getting a new heart too." She squeezed Di's shoulder and whispered in her ear. "I thought you said you were no good with a needle and thread."

Di held up her bandaged thumb. "It took some effort but totally worth it."

22

A crowd gathered outside the doors to the Fine Arts building as Di and family arrived for the dedication of Eva's Garden. July was not the best time to schedule an outdoor ceremony, especially with the mid-morning temperature already hitting ninety degrees. At least the program would be short, and with summer break, no passing students would distract.

Aunt Glori leaned close and muttered in Di's ear. "Did you get a chance to mix her ashes into the dirt?"

"It's all taken care of." Di wiped away the drop of sweat sliding down the side of her face.

The sunflower mural to one side of the entrance proved an attention-grabber with its bright yellows and oranges contrasting against brown centers and green leaves and stems. Away from the building's front doors, a mature crape myrtle's hot pink crown provided welcome shade for a wrought iron bench. The sight of two of Eva's former neighbors occupying the seat made Di smile. She recognized a couple of her mother's fellow professors strolling the pave-stone pathway winding between blue plumbagoes, pink antique roses, and multi-colored portulaca. A plaque at the front read "Eva Malone Memorial Garden."

Mitch pointed to a round base next to the plaque. "What's going in there?"

"I don't know. I thought we had everything finished." Di turned to Julianna. "What did we forget?"

Julianna gave a one-shoulder shrug, her attention never straying from whatever fascination her phone held.

Dr. Lynne Arquette, the Art Department chair, called to Di above the friendly chatter and hurried toward her. "We're about to get started, but could you stay a few minutes afterward? I have something for you in my office."

"Of course. By the way, this is my husband, Mitch. You've met Julianna"—Di looked around—"who seems to have disappeared. Where did she go?"

"She went to meet Namiko." Aunt Glori introduced herself and shook hands with Dr. Arquette.

"She's Aunt Glori to us," Di added. "She and Eva were best friends since their college days."

"Very nice to meet you both," Dr. Arquette said. "Isabella and Noah, who did the artwork on the mural, are around here somewhere. I hope you're pleased with their efforts."

"I love it. It's so vibrant and lifelike." Di nodded toward the empty base. "May I ask what's going—" She never got a chance to finish the question.

Professor Arquette strode away, took a microphone in hand, and stood next to the memorial garden marker, shading her eyes from the bright sunlight. "Good morning and welcome. I'd like to thank you all for coming to this dedication of the Eva Malone Memorial Garden. I had the privilege of working with Eva during her last year before she retired. She was a talented artist and a wonderful lady. It's been a pleasure to work with her daughter and granddaughter on this project. We have one final touch to add to the garden this morning." She gestured to someone at the rear of the audience.

Di's mouth fell open when Noah appeared, pushing a dolly carrying Eva's vase to the front. Namiko helped him position it on the platform. Golden veins, gleaming in the bright sunlight, streaked through the neck and sides of the vase where the broken pieces were melded together. In place of a useless, fragmented piece of pottery stood a beautiful work of art.

Di swallowed past the lump in her throat and grabbed Mitch's arm, squeezing it with both hands. Eva would have loved this.

Dr. Arquette continued. "I understand this vase earned Eva her first award as an artist. An unfortunate accident resulted in several fractures. However, Namiko Ito here saw the potential beauty in its flaws and asked permission to repair it. Employing the ancient Japanese art of *kintsugi*, he put the broken pieces together again, highlighting the imperfections rather than hiding them. When we learned of his work, it seemed fitting to give it a proper home here in Eva's memorial garden."

Applause rippled through the audience.

Julianna set up a tablet-sized solar panel nearby. Isabella uncoiled the cord attached to the solar cell and handed the end to Noah, who worked behind the vase. Moments later, he nodded to Namiko and soon a plume of water rose from the center of the vase, reaching several inches above the rim before cascading down into the bowl.

A fountain! If only Eva could see this.

Dr. Arquette gestured to her. "Diamond Lange, would you like to say a few words?"

Di was too choked up to speak, but Mitch and Aunt Glori pushed her toward the front. She took the microphone from the professor and allowed herself several deep breaths. She looked out on Eva's friends, colleagues, and likely a few of her former students.

"Thanks to each of you for coming out this morning to honor my mother. I can't tell you how much it means to me, and I know it would mean even more to her. I was excited about the garden, but this—" She looked the fountain over and nearly burst with delight.

Shifting her gaze to the four young people, she continued. "You have no idea how this touches my heart. My mother—Eva—used to say there's beauty in everything, but not everyone can see it. Namiko, thank you for sharing with us the value to be found in a worthless, broken vase." She could still feel the heartsick ache at seeing the fractured pieces on the lawn and driveway. Never did she imagine seeing it like this.

"I don't know who came up with the fountain idea, but it's wonderful. Isabella and Noah," she turned toward the mural, "your sunflowers will brighten even the dreariest day on campus."

Di faced the crowd again and held her hand out toward the four students. "My daughter, Julianna, gets credit for the idea of a memorial garden. She inherited Eva's creative spirit and enjoyed an especially close relationship with her." How could she have once envied their bond? What a privilege for both daughter and grandmother.

"And finally, Dr. Arquette, my deepest gratitude to you and the university for allowing us to honor my mother in this way." With a nod to the professor, Di tried to recall her planned closing remarks, but they eluded her. She managed to croak, "Thank you all," before handing the microphone to Dr. Arquette, who finished the program and dismissed the crowd.

Misty Ballard wheeled her dad through the departing guests to greet Di.

"This is spectacular," Ed said. "Fits Eva perfectly."

Di noted he was wearing his ring. "Thank you so much for coming."

"Wouldn't have missed it." He took her hand, his fingers stiff and bony but palm soft and warm. "Don't be a stranger now. Come and see me when you have time to chat."

Di promised to visit and as others stepped up to speak with her, she caught sight of Scott talking with Mitch. Their eyes met, and Scott touched his hat in salute, winked, and gave her a thumbs up.

Julianna appeared at her side as the crowd thinned out. "We surprised you, didn't we?" She bobbed on her toes with a face-splitting grin.

Di pulled her into a hug, then reached to include Namiko. "How did you—"

"Easy." Julianna stepped back. "After you and I met with Dr. Arquette, I only had to contact her and explain what we wanted to do. She loved the idea and promised to keep it a secret."

"The fountain was Julianna's idea," Namiko said, "after she saw what I was doing with the vase. I like the way it adds movement and life to something inanimate."

"Exactly," Di said. "You never met Eva, did you?"

"No, I'm sorry, but Julianna speaks highly of her. I think she and I would have had much in common."

Dr. Arquette beckoned, and Di excused herself. She caught up with the professor at the door of the building and sighed with pleasure at the cool air inside.

Leading the way to her second-floor office, Dr. Arquette waved her arm in an expansive gesture. "We've been doing a lot of cleaning."

"That's something I love to hear."

"So many projects get left behind at the end of the year.

Over time, they accumulate. Our priority this summer is to clean out everything that doesn't pertain to our current class program." She unlocked her door and went to her desk.

Di couldn't help but compare the cluttered office to Eva's house, right up to the framed abstract art hanging on the walls. Eva always maintained that creativity was messy. This office gave proof to that theory.

"We found this." Dr. Arquette pulled a canvas from behind her desk and held it for Di to see. "It's very different from any of Eva's other paintings, but I thought you would want it."

Di inhaled sharply. The star painting. She stared at the illustration of a woman on tiptoes under a night sky, the Milky Way prominent amid the star-studded canopy. A kerchief covered her hair, and a feather duster sprouted from her pocket. In one upraised hand she held a glowing orb while a cloth hung from her other hand, as if she were polishing a star. A chain encircling her neck held a sparkling gem.

Her diamond necklace? The duster and cleaning rag—Eva had chosen to portray her as a cleaning woman.

Di's heart shattered into a million pieces.

But wait. Eva could have painted a dusty, chaotic scene, the way the neighborhood looked after the tornado. This whole scene possessed a dreamy, heartwarming quality. A cleaning woman reaching into the sky to pluck the stars from their places?

"What do you think?" Dr. Arquette smiled, obviously pleased.

"It's . . . ." Di struggled for an appropriate response. "I don't know what to say."

"Once I saw Eva's signature on it, I recalled your necklace and knew this was her tribute to you. She was obviously proud of you."

Di mentally shook her head. "What makes you think that? I

mean—" Heat flushed her neck and cheeks. She wasn't fishing for compliments. "I'm afraid I didn't inherit Eva's artistic genes. I don't know the first thing about interpreting art. Tell me what you see."

Dr. Arquette moved to Di's side and turned the painting so they could both see it. "She's standing on tiptoes stretching toward the starry sky, reaching beyond the common and mundane, beyond what most of us strive for."

The professor pointed to the orb. "Polishing a star with its glowing, magical quality is a lofty, majestic task. She's adding light and beauty to the world, also represented by the sparkling necklace. Stars are often described as diamonds on the black velvet of a night sky. Both stars and diamonds speak of value and great worth."

Like magnets, her words pulled the pieces of Di's fractured heart together, melding them with gold as precious as Namiko's *kintsugi*. She took the painting in her hands and whispered a hoarse, "Thank you."

"My pleasure. I'm glad we had a chance to meet so I could pass this on to you. It's a good thing I noticed Eva's signature before we disposed of it." Dr. Arquette put a hand on her shoulder as they walked toward the door. "I need to stay and work on a few things. Are you able to find your way out?"

"Yes, thank you."

Di kept a tight hold on the stairway railing to guide her down the steps. Her vision blurred with unshed tears. At the bottom, she wiped her eyes and stared at the painting that was almost thrown out as trash. She too had considered everything trash—the doll, the piano, the vase. Yet each was treasured by someone whose love gave it value and worth.

Mitch called to her from the door. "Diamond? Ready to go?"

"Coming." She lifted her chin, threw her shoulders back, and strode toward him.

Mitch held the door for her. "Whatcha got? Is that the last of the worthless treasures?" He craned his neck for a peek.

"They were all treasures. But worthless? Never. More like priceless."

AFTERWORD

Follow this link for a peek at what Eva's star painting might have looked like: https://tinyurl.com/yc8pmrkw

If you enjoyed this book, please recommend it to friends. Word of mouth is powerful. Leaving an honest review on the purchase site and/or on Goodreads.com will be helpful for other readers like you. Thanks so much!

Learn more about Mary L Hamilton's books by subscribing to her monthly newsletter. Go to https://maryhamiltonbooks.com/ and scroll to the bottom.

ACKNOWLEDGMENTS

This book couldn't have been written without help and support. I especially want to thank Jennifer Snyder of Neat As A Pin in Waco, TX for her expertise as a professional cleaner and organizer. Any inaccuracies or "poetic license" should be attributed to me. Thank you, Jennifer, for your time and willingness to educate me as to your profession.

For medical matters, thanks go to Dr. Ronda Wells who coached me on matters pertaining to pediatric heart transplants, and to Liberty Adair for her knowledge of emergency department procedures. The information you both shared plays a huge part in this story. I'm also indebted to Deanna Schiesser for her willingness to share her daughter's transplant story.

I can't thank my Team Barnabas critique group enough. The story was stuck until I began meeting with these fellow writers. Their constructive advice and encouragement kept me plowing through. Y'all are the best!

Thank you to Montra Weaver for her editing skills, but most of all for her encouragement and friendship as I worked on this story.

My daughter, Beki Allen, serves as a sounding board for ideas and is my first reader, making suggestions and catching flaws before I send the manuscript to an editor. In addition, my husband, Wayne, helps me sort out problems and situations. Much appreciation goes not only to Beki and Wayne but to my whole family for their constant interest and support. You'll never know how much it means to me.

Most of all, I give thanks to Jesus Christ, the author of my salvation and lover of my soul, who has gifted me with the ability to write. This I offer back to Him as worship.

ABOUT THE AUTHOR

Texas author Mary L. Hamilton writes contemporary fiction rippled with faith. She finds inspiration for her novels in real-life situations. If you know her personally, be careful or you may end up in one of her books. In addition to writing, she enjoys reading, knitting, and quiet evenings at home with her husband and her dog. You can learn more at https://maryhamiltonbooks.com/. Even better, join her newsletter crew for monthly updates and a personal column by her dog, Cinder.

Other books by Mary L. Hamilton

Dead Air: A Waco Mystery
Pendant (mystery/suspense under pen name M L Hamilton)
Rustic Knoll Bible Camp series (For young teens and those who think like young teens)
    Hear No Evil, Book 1
    Speak No Evil, Book 2
    See No Evil, Book 3

DISCUSSION QUESTIONS

1. The title, *Worthless Treasures*, suggests a contradiction. From your reading of the novel, explain what it might mean. What relation do you see to the themes of the story?

2. Diamond is a pro at decluttering and helping people discard things they no longer need. Why do you think her mother's belongings pose such a struggle for her? Discuss any similar challenges you've faced.

3. What value does Diamond place on the five objects from Eva's list? How does that perception change over the course of the novel? Were you surprised at any of the objects' stories?

4. From the beginning, Diamond doubts her own worth. How does dealing with Eva's house help her realize what is truly valuable in life?

5. What do you own that holds weighty sentimental value, though it has little or no monetary worth? Why is it important to you?

6. In what ways do Diamond and Eva misunderstand each other? Do you think Eva truly saw and appreciated Diamond for who she was?

7. Julianna has a much closer relationship with Eva than her mother does. Why do you think they connected so well? Would the contrast with Diamond's experience growing up have any bearing on that?

8. Scott Jones makes an unexpected return to Diamond's life. Initially, what does he represent to her? How does her perception of him change as the novel progresses?

9. While Mitch is a steady, supportive husband, Diamond still feels the temptation toward Scott. Do you think she ever truly considers rekindling something with Scott? Why or why not?

10. What influence does Lyndee Rae exert in Diamond's journey? How does their friendship impact Diamond's understanding of what it means to treasure something—or someone?

11. The story includes different kinds of loss—the loss of a parent, the loss of a home, and even the impending loss of a child. What does the book say about grief and resilience?

12. Why do you think Eva kept so many things? Was she truly a hoarder? Did she have deeper reasons for her attachment to certain objects?

13. Do you think Diamond honored Eva's last wishes in the way she "passed on" the items? Would Eva have been pleased?

14. How do Diamond's views of her own value change from the beginning to the end? What message does that ultimately convey about our own self-worth?

15. Did you find the ending satisfying? Did Diamond find the closure she needed?

16. If you could ask the author one question about the book, what would it be?

17. What idea did you take away from this story? Has it prompted you to rethink how you view sentimental objects or relationships?